I0526985

# Aiden Branss presents:
# The Legend Of Evil Murphy

The Resistance

. Library of Congress Control Number:

2023946159

ISBN: 978-2-8372-9228-5

**AidenBranssBooks.com**

*The world is a dangerous place to live, not because of the people who are evil, but because of the people who don't do anything about it.*

- **ALBERT EINSTEIN**

# 30 YEARS iN ThE FUTURE

*In a desolate world, ravaged by the tyranny of Murphy, a young adult named Randy and his valiant commander, Damaris, fought alongside their friend, Ms. Garcia, as members of "The Resistance." Murphy was an evil dictator ruling with an iron fist, he had brought the world to its knees, and destruction was imminent. As bombs rained down from the darkened sky, Randy, Damaris, and Ms. Garcia sprinted through the chaos. This was their last chance to stop Murphy's reign of terror.*

*Randy: "Ms. Garcia!"*

*Ms. Garcia: "Yes Randy?!"*

*Randy: "Damaris has been shot! He's hurt bad!"*

*Damaris was in an immense amount of pain! He was looking down at his bleeding wound.*

*Commander Damaris: "Damn! Murphy's army sure is a hassle!"*

*He clenched his hand in agony as the pain got worse. They all jumped in a trench nearby and hid while Randy started to clean the commanders wound. Bombs kept falling from the sky, and Murphy's vicious soldiers were on foot, in tanks, and were zooming through the sky in planes! There was no hope left in sight.*

*Ms. Garcia: "Commander, what do we do?"*

*Randy: "There's way too many of them!"*

*Commander Damaris: "Face it gang, The Resistance failed. Murphy won."*

*The world was crumbling down around them. The devastation Murphy sought for, had come to fruition. All hope was lost.*

*Ms. Garcia: "Commander, we can't just give up!"*

*Randy: "What can we do?"*

*Commander Damaris: "There's nothing we can do..."*

*All hope seemed lost, until...*

*Commander Damaris: "Wait- there is something we have that Murphy and his troops don't have... hope."*

*Randy and Ms. Garcia were confused.*

*Commander Damaris: "Ms. Garcia, remember a few years ago when we looted Murphy's headquarters and found that prototype...?"*

*She knew exactly what he was talking about! She dove into her backpack and pulled out a metal, bright device.*

*Ms. Garcia: "Isn't this the... Damaris, are you sure about this?"*

*Randy stood there puzzled.*

*Commander Damaris: "Yes I am, it is the only way..."*

*When he said that, a shiny light coming from one of the planes in the sky pointed down directly at them in the trench! Over a loud intercom they heard the plane send out an alert!*

*"ALERT! ALL UNITS, WE HAVE DETECTED THE FINAL RESISTANCE MEMBERS IN A TRENCH!"*

*Ms. Garcia: "SHOOT!"*

*Ms. Garcia knew the idea Damaris had, was their last chance for victory. The last chance, to save the world. She looked over at Randy and began to tear up a bit. She went up to him and gave him a hug.*

*Ms. Garcia: "I'll hold them off, you got this Randy!"*

*She pulled out her blaster gun. and jumped out of the trench. She was ready to fight until her very last breath. Randy of course, was very confused!*

*Randy: "Okay, what the hell is going on?!"*

*Commander Damaris: "Listen to me very closely..."*

*He started to fidget with the weird device.*

*Commander Damaris: "A few years back, Murphy had begun development of a device that can send people throughout time."*

*Randy: "WAIT WHAT?"*

**Commander Damaris: "I know it's crazy. They built this prototype of a time machine, but luckily, we stole it before they ever tested it. Who knows what he would have done with a powerful device like this!"**

**Ms. Garcia was standing near the trench when an army of troops came rushing at her.**

**Ms. Garcia: "They're coming!"**

**Both of the men heard her.**

**Commander Damaris: "We don't have much time!"**

**He put his hand on Randy's shoulder.**

**Commander Damaris: "We have to send you back in time."**

**Randy: "What the hell?!"**

**Ms. Garcia started to avoid the shots coming from Murphy's army! She started firing her blaster at them like crazy!**

**Ms. Garcia: "Bring it on assholes!"**

**She ran closer to the army and took each of them out, one by one.**

**Commander Damaris: "Listen Randy!"**

**Randy began to panic.**

*Commander Damaris: "This is the only way we can prevent any of this from happening!"*

*Commander Damaris: "30 years ago, Murphy's invasion began, and this is our only hope left!"*

*The commander started to turn the device on. Meanwhile, Ms. Garcia almost took out the last of the Murphy troopers, until a man came flying down at her! He was wearing a jetpack and zoomed down towards her! She jumped out of the way and shot him down midair, and he fell to the ground hard. She rushed over to the man and ripped the jetpack off his body. She ran over to the trench and threw the jetpack at Randy.*

*Ms. Garcia: "You are going to need this!"*

*The weight of the world was on Randy's shoulders. The trooper who fell looked over at Ms. Garcia and said...*

*"He's coming for you."*

*She kicked in his face! Then suddenly, a giant ship in the sky emerged from out of nowhere.*

*Ms. Garcia: "Holy shit, he's here!"*

*The commander and Randy noticed the ship.*

*Randy: "He found us!"*

*The commander turned on the device, and it began slowly powering on.*

*Commander Damaris: "SHIT! This damn thing better hurry up!"*

*The ship in the sky projected down a large bright beam right near the trench. Ms. Garcia knew exactly who was coming...*

*Commander Damaris: "Listen to me very carefully, I'm sending you back to when I was a teenager. You need to stop Murphy before he becomes way too powerful! Do it, before it's too late!"*

*Randy was scared and felt panicked, but he knew it had to be done.*

*Commander Damaris: "One last thing."*

*Randy: "Yes commander?"*

*Commander Damaris: "There is only one person I knew who can prevent this..."*

*Randy: "Who?!"*

*Commander Damaris: "Find my friend known as The Author. He's the only person I knew who can stop this war from happening!"*

*The beam of light had gotten brighter, and a shadow could be seen emerging through the glare...*

*Ms. Garcia: "Bring it on you bastard!"*

*Walking out through the bright beam of light, was Murphy.*

*Murphy: "Well if it isn't the last of The Resistance, I just had to see it for myself."*

*Ms. Garcia: "I'M GOING TO KILL YOU!"*

*Murphy had a grim look on his face.*

*Murphy: "You are welcome to try."*

*She ran at him full force...*

*From the trenches, all Randy and Damaris heard was a loud gunshot...*

*Commander Damaris: "Dear God, no..."*

*He peeked his head out of the trench and saw his beloved friend, dead. The commander was filled with rage!*

*Commander Damaris: "I'll hold him off, goodbye Randy, I know you'll make us proud."*

*They took one last look at each other, and the commander jumped out of the trench to face his nemesis. Randy began pressing all the buttons on the device in a hurry!*

*Commander Damaris: "MURPHY!"*

*Murphy turned around with a menacing grin on his face.*

Murphy: "Well, look who it is... After all these years Damaris, I can't wait to finally kill you, just like I did to all your little friends."

Damaris grabbed his blaster and looked Murphy directly in the eyes...

Commander Damaris: "They were your friends also you dick!"

The commander shot at Murphy, and he dodged it. Murphy cracked his knuckles and slowly walked toward Damaris. Meanwhile in the trench, Randy was in a hurry to activate the device!

Randy: "Shit, shit, shit! Please work!"

To his surprise it started to work! On the device there was a little screen that said, "Select Destination" and it had a dial on it. Randy turned back the dial, and, on the screen, it said, "Travel Back 30 Years?" and he clicked the confirm button! The screen said, "Please wait, processing."

Randy: "Hurry the fuck up!"

Above the trench, Murphy was pounding Damaris in the face with his fist. His blood was splattered all over Murphy's superhuman body. He then threw Damaris to the ground and spit on him.

Murphy: "Damaris, the war is over, I won."

*Damaris turned his broken body over to stare at the trench. The machine had begun to latch onto Randy and his entire body started to glow yellow!*

*Randy: "Oh shit what's happening?!"*

*The commander turned his head to look back at Murphy, he then swiftly grabbed a knife from his back pocket, and he shanked it right in Murphy's ankle!*

*Murphy: "AHHHHH!"*

*Commander Damaris: "You are so wrong Murphy, THIS WAR IS NOT OVER!"*

*Murphy looked over at the trench and saw Randy indulged in the yellow light. Randy looked at the device and screamed out loud!*

*Randy: "Damaris it says 10 seconds till send off!"*

*Murphy: "OH NO YOU DON'T!"*

*Murphy sprinted towards the trench! But Damaris got up and tackled Murphy to the ground with the little amount of strength he had left in him. The light consumed Randy more and his body began to vanish into the light!*

*Randy: "THIS IS CRAZY!"*

*Murphy stood up and he grabbed Damaris by the neck.*

*Damaris: "Fuck, you."*

*Murphy: "You'll pay for that, with your life!"*

*What happened next traumatized Randy. As Murphy was holding Damaris by the neck, all Randy heard was a loud crack sound... his whole body went limp, and Murphy threw his body down in the trench next to him.*

*Randy: "NOOOOO!"*

*Murphy jumped into the trench, and he took one small step. Randy thought he was next, when suddenly, he vanished into thin air! Murphy stood there, worried about what was to come.*

*Murphy: "So, they were the ones who stole my time travel machine!?"*

*He reached for his walkie talkie and sent a message out.*

*Murphy: "Troops! This war, is far from over!"*

*He threw down the walkie talkie into the dirt.*

*Murphy: "This is so far from over..."*

\*\*\*\*\*\*\*\*\*\*\*\*\*\*\*\*\*\*\*\*\*\*\*\*\*\*\*\*\*\*\*\*\*\*\*\*\*\*\*\*\*\*\*\*\*\*\*\*\*\*\*\*\*\*\*\*\*\*\*\*\*\*\*\*\*\*\*\*\*\*\*\*\*

*In the middle of the night, in a suburban town, a glowing orb emerged from out of nowhere. The orb grew, and it grew huge! The light projecting from it was so bright, but nobody was in sight. Suddenly, it formed into a portal, and Randy came jumping out*

16

*of it! He was in great distress, breathing heavily, with a traumatized look on his face after seeing two of his friends die. He was in shock. He had just successfully traveled back in time.*

*Randy: "Oh God. Oh God."*

# MONDay

**The Author was an 18-year-old boy, and around this time, he was worried about his high school graduation that was approaching in just a few days. This one morning he was writing in his journal.**

*"In just a few days, my friends and I will all be going off into the real world, and we all will split up and move on with our lives..."*

**While he was deep in his feelings, his phone started ringing. He picked up the phone, and it was one of his close homies calling. Kids in their school would always give this kid a disrespectful attitude, and some would make fun of him for his height. He's 3'2 tall at 18 years old, and his name is The Short Kid. The two of them met in 9th grade, and since then, they have become very close. The Author picked up the phone, and Short Kid sounded frantic!**

**Short Kid: "AUTHOR!"**

**He shouted in his ear!**

**Author: "WHAT!"**

**The Author thought to himself "Why is he screaming? Something must be wrong."**

**Author: "Short Kid, what's wrong?"**

**The next few words he heard, turned his face bright tomato red.**

**Short Kid: "I bought you a vape!"**

*Author put down the phone for a second and reconsidered his sadness about losing his friends. In his head he thought, "Maybe moving on with life isn't such a bad thing after all?"*

*Author: \*Sigh\**

*Author: "May I ask why?"*

*Short Kid: "Well, two things. First, I wanted to celebrate the success of your new book!"*

*Author: "What's the second reason?"*

*Short Kid: "WE ARE GRADUATING SATURDAY!"*

*Author: "Thanks for reminding me..."*

*Short Kid: "Come on just take the vape, it'll be fun! We can smoke our vapes together until they get empty!"*

*He thought about it and realized that it's the thought of the gift that counts. So, he accepted the generous gesture.*

*Author: "Thank you Short Kid."*

*Short Kid: "Yeah, no problem champ."*

*Author: "When can I get it?"*

*Short Kid: "Oh, I'm actually standing outside your house right now!"*

*The Author looked out his window and saw Short Kid standing there smiling and waving!*

*Short Kid: "You see me bro? I see you!"*

*Author: "Yeah, I see you. I'll be right down."*

*He hung up the phone and headed downstairs and out the door. He got outside and Short Kid was so happy to see him!*

*Short Kid: "Author, you are going to love this!"*

*Author: "We'll see about that."*

*He pulled it out, and at first, he thought nothing of it. It just looked like any other vape he had ever seen.*

*Author: "Thanks, it looks so unique?"*

*Short Kid: "Author, trust me. You want this."*

*The Author was so confused, Short Kid seemed very persistent on him liking the vape.*

*Author: "Short Kid, what's the big deal? It looks like just a normal vape bro."*

*Short Kid: "Author…"*

*Short Kid: "It's a coffee flavored vape!"*

*Once he said that, The Author's jaw dropped and hit the ground! He snatched it out of The Short Kid's hand and held it like a piece of gold!*

*Author: "Oh my..."*

*Author: "It's beautiful!"*

*If you can't tell, he really likes coffee. He says he loves it so much and that it's by far the best drink ever created. Some say he has an addiction, but personally he thinks of it as an innocent obsession. Anyway, he thanked Short Kid and gave him a fist pump, because he was so grateful for the gift. Short Kid said he had to leave to go somewhere, so The Author went back inside his house. He put the vape under his pillowcase to save it in case there was ever a special occasion. The Author laid back down in his bed and started to talk out loud.*

*Author: "Wow, that was sure nice of him to bring me this. I wonder where he had to go?"*

*He then checked his alarm clock, and it said it was 9 AM!*

*Author: "OH HAMBURGERS, I AM SO LATE FOR SCHOOL!"*

*He grabbed his backpack filled with empty mint wrappers and called Short Kid to come back to give him a ride to school!*

*Short Kid: "My bad."*

*Later that day, The Author and his friend decided to leave campus and go out for lunch. His friend's name is Murphy. They have been best friends since they were toddlers. Yeah, they go way back.*

*The Author would always say to people "Murphy is the type of guy to never switch up on you or stab you in the back. He's just that good of a guy. I'd be surprised if he ever did something out of line." During their lunch break, they were eating inside of a Burger Queen. The Author was drinking a coffee and Murphy had a mango smoothie with some onion rings as they were discussing life.*

*Author: "Life is moving so fast, like our graduation is only a few days away!"*

*Murphy: "Time flies fast Author. It sure does feel like just yesterday we were little kids playing at the park."*

*When he said that, The Author felt those nostalgic memories. He wished he could go back to those simpler times.*

*Author: "If only time travel was real bro."*

*Murphy: "Yeah, it's sad, but trust me dude when I say this. We are going to make a bunch of fun new memories in the future dude, remember that business we always wanted to start?!"*

*Author: "Yeah, I remember..."*

*Murphy: "Say it..."*

*Author: "The corn dog business."*

*Murphy: "YES! I can't wait till we get that running up!"*

*They always wanted to start crazy businesses together growing up. For example, one time when they were kids, they tried to start a toenail clipping business. Unsurprisingly, that business failed.*

*Author: "Don't stress dude, we will for sure start a successful company or organization someday!"*

*Murphy: "Author, you already are successful with the books though! You have inspired me to work hard bro, I want to be rich, and famous, and powerful someday!"*

*Author: "I appreciate that."*

*Murphy: "Someday, I want to be just like my grandpa, but better than him…"*

*Murphy's grandfather was a very well-known local. The Author had never met him, but he always heard great stories about him. Murphy's grandpa is a multi-millionaire! He made tons of money back in the 80s, and he uses his fortune for good. Murphy's grandpa has opened homeless shelters and orphanages all over the state, and there is even one shelter he owns that is in the town they live in. He was known by the public as a very good man.*

*Author: "Murphy, you will be like him, but it would be dope if I got to meet him sometime!"*

*As they were talking, they both check their phones and realized they had been sitting in the fast-food establishment for over an hour!*

*Murphy: "Uh oh!"*

*Author: "DUDE!"*

*Author: "Our lunch break ended over a 45 minutes ago!"*

*I don't know how they didn't notice! I guess when you're having a deep talk, time goes by faster. They left in a hurry and started heading back to school. But they weren't in a rush to get back or anything like that, so they took their time slowly walking.*

*Author: "Man, we are going to be nagged by the attendance lady, again."*

*Murphy: "Good, I love the thrill of trouble."*

*As they were walking, The Author's phone started ringing. He took it out and saw he was getting a FaceTime call...*

*Author: "Oh shit, my girl is calling!"*

*He picked up the phone right away.*

*Author: "Hey Riley, what's up?"*

*Riley: "Bae, where are you? The dean's administration is looking for you!"*

*Author: "Darn, okay, I'm walking there now, Murphy and I went out for lunch, and we were talking."*

*Riley: "Oh can he hear me?! HI MURPHY!"*

*They all laughed because of how loud she screamed that over the phone!*

*Murphy: "Hi, ha-ha."*

*Author: "I'll be there in a few minutes."*

*Riley: "Okay, I love you."*

*The Author blushed.*

*Author: "I love you more."*

*Riley: "I love you most."*

*Author: "Ok bye Ri."*

*They ended the phone call.*

*Murphy: "AWWWW! Ya'll are such an adorable couple!"*

*Author: "Oh Murphy, shut up."*

*Murphy: "I just wish I was loved like that by someone, anybody really."*

*The Author thought it was a bit strange he said that. But before he could really think about it, his phone started ringing, again.*

*Author: "Who the heck is calling me now?"*

*He checked his phone and now this local politician lady he knew was calling him. Her name is Linda, but everyone refers to her as Ms. Garcia. They met each other the year before. She was running for some elected office in their town, and The Author met her at a coffee shop and since then, they have become good friends. She has also been helping him make connections with certain people and businesses to help boost his writing career. He had a feeling that her calling him meant that she had to tell him something super important, so he answered the phone right away!*

*Author: "Hey!"*

*Ms. Garcia: "Hello Mr. Author, it's excellent to be speaking with you again."*

*Author: "It's good to be chatting with you too! Look, I am going to take a wild guess, you are calling me to tell me something cool, right?"*

*He could hear her laughing on the other side of the phone.*

*Ms. Garcia: "Well, I hope you consider it cool! I'm calling you to let you know about an event happening this evening..."*

*He was already super intrigued, and so was Murphy, they both put their ears up to the phone and listened closely to her next few words.*

*Ms. Garcia: "Tonight, a bunch of senators, representatives, and businessmen and women are gathering at a banquet hall, and guess what..."*

*Author: "What?!"*

*Ms. Garcia: "I got you a ticket inside!"*

*He threw a fist pump up in the air when she said that!*

*Ms. Garcia: "It's an invite only type of thing, and I convinced the higher ups to let you come in!"*

*Author: "WOW, thank you so much! I will definitely be there!"*

*Ms. Garcia: "I didn't even get to tell you the best part!"*

*Author: "What's the best part?"*

*Ms. Garcia: "After hours of negotiating with these people..."*

*Author: "Damn, hours?"*

*Ms. Garcia: "Haha, okay more like 5 minutes, I was able to get you an extra ticket inside the venue!"*

*When she said that, he got so happy and excited!*

*Author: "Thank you so much Ms. G! How can I ever repay you?"*

*Ms. Garcia: "Don't worry about it, just come well dressed with your guest and be there at 6 PM."*

*Author: "You got it!"*

*Ms. Garcia: "Great, I'm going to tell the newspaper you'll be attending, see you then, Author!"*

*She hung up the phone, and Author was so eager and excited! He looked over at Murphy and smiled.*

*Author: "Bro, did you hear what she just said?!"*

*Murphy: "Good stuff my man!"*

*Author: "DUDE! She said she got me an extra ticket inside! Do you want to come with me?"*

*Murphy: "I'm sorry Author, I would, but to be fair, one day, I will be better than all those people, so it doesn't matter."*

*Author: "Oh."*

*Murphy: "Also, I promised my brother I would teach him how to roll a blunt."*

*Author really wanted him to come with, and he thought it was super odd what he just said about being better than those people. But he just played it off as a joke.*

*Murphy: "Dude, I just realized something."*

*Author: "What's up?"*

*Murphy: "We are over 2 hours late to class!"*

*Author: "Damn, well we should probably hurry up then!"*

*So, they rushed back to school, but first The Author stopped for a latte. Then after being 3 hours late, The Author got into the building, and the second he took one step through those doors, all eyes were on him… Tons of kids from his school have read his books and well, a lot of students and teachers considered him controversial. As he walked further into the building, he heard some kid booing at him, and another gave him the middle finger. But The Author didn't care that much. He thought to himself "I'm going to be hanging out with senators tonight, while that kid is probably going to be on his phone looking at air fryer recipes."*
*He was also walking slowly through the hallways trying not to get noticed by any teachers or staff.*

*Author: "Shit, I've been tardy to way too many classes lately, If I can just avoid this administration for just a few more days, I'm in the clear."*

*He got to his class without trouble and sat down at a desk. He put his head down and put in his $3 headphones. He went through the rest of the school day bored out of his mind. The rest of the day he kept asking himself "Who should I bring with me to the event?" He thought about it for a bit, but it clicked in his head. He knew exactly who to bring.*

*Author: "Wait duh, I'll ask my girl."*

*At the end of the school day, He stood outside waiting for his sweetheart. It was extremely sunny, and all the kids were excited to be out of school for the day. As he was waiting outside, someone came up to him and asked him to sign a copy of one of his books. They handed it to him, and he wrote them a nice little message.*

*Author: "Here you go bro."*

*The random kid said, "Thanks dude, I love this book, even though my dad hates you, anyway bye!"*

*Author: "Oh okay, thanks?"*

*Then the kid walked off. The Author turned around and saw tons of random kids walking out of the school, he had no clue who any of them were, and he didn't care to know. But then, he saw deep within the crowd, there she was. His whole attention was focused on her, He didn't even pay attention to the other 100 kids rushing and pushing past him. She walked up to him, and he saw her amazing smile.*

*Author: "Hey Riley!"*

*Riley: "You are so lucky the principal didn't catch you today!"*

*Author: "Screw that guy, we'll be out of here in a few days anyway, and I'll never have to deal with him again."*

*She smiled and gave him a hug, and then she smacked his butt!*

*Author: "RILEY!"*

*Author: "DON'T DO THAT, ESPECIALLY IN PUBLIC!"*

*Riley: "Sorry, dragul meu."*

*Author: "You know, sometimes I forget your Romanian."*

*Riley: "Do you like that?"*

*The Author smiled and he walked Riley to her bus.*

*Author: "Hey I was going to ask if tonight you want to come with me…"*

*Riley: "I can't."*

*Author: "I didn't even get to finish my sentence!"*

*Riley: "I know, I'd want to come with for whatever it is, but tonight is my sister's birthday party."*

*Author: "Oh yeah I forgot about Tesla's birthday party at the arcade."*

*Riley: "Author, we've been over this several times, her name is Tessa, not Tesla!"*

*Author: "Oh yeah, I forgot."*

*She grabbed his hand.*

*Riley: "Listen, you should ask Natasha if she wants to go with you."*

*Author: "That's true."*

*Riley: "She would appreciate the company."*

*Author: "Yeah I guess."*

*Bus Driver: "Hurry up, get on the damn bus!"*

*Riley: "Oh, I have to go, call me tonight!"*

*She started to walk on the bus and blew a kiss to The Author!*

*Author: "I WILL!"*

*The doors closed on the bus, and it began to drive off. The couple looked at each other through the window until the moment they could not see each other anymore.*

*Author: "She's so awesome."*

*He whipped out his phone and called their mutual friend Natasha to ask if she would be down to come with him to the event. He knew that she was having a hard time coping with high school coming to an end, and he wanted to raise her spirits a bit. He called and she picked up the phone fast.*

*Author: "Hello?"*

*Natasha: "Hey man."*

*He filled her in on all the details.*

*Author: "Would you be down to come with me?"*

*She paused for a moment.*

*Natasha: "Sure, screw it."*

*Author: "Bet, come to my house at like 5 so we can be ready on time!"*

*Natasha: "Sounds good Author."*

*He told her about some of the people who would be attending the event. She seemed excited but also a bit anxious. The Author reassured her everything would be okay. He hung up the phone and put his crappy headphones in while he waited for his mom to come pick him up from school...*

*******************************************************************

*Randy was walking down a street in the middle of town.*

*Randy: "Damn it!"*

*He was frustrated.*

*Randy: "How the hell am I supposed to find any of these people?"*

*He sat down on a bench.*

*Randy: "FUCK! Why did Damaris trust me this much... there's no way I'm going to be able to prevent the future."*

*He felt hopeless.*

*Randy: "If only I could find a clue."*

*He sat there and was feeling like a loser, when he saw a man walk past reading a newspaper. The man said something out loud.*

*"This paper is junk, fake news!"*

*He threw the newspaper in a nearby trashcan. He walked past Randy huffing and puffing. Randy stood up to go retrieve the paper from the trash.*

*Randy: "Junk? These people are so lucky, and don't even know it, I wish in the future we had newspapers!"*

*He picked up the paper and began to read it. It was boring at first until a headline caught his attention that read...*

*Breaking News: State Senators and Local Politicians to Attend Exclusive Event Tonight*

*He began to read the article...*

"Tonight, a group of prominent state senators, local politicians and businessmen and women are set to gather tonight at the prestigious banquet hall for a highly anticipated event. This exclusive affair promises to be an evening filled with notable personalities and captivating discussions.

Among the special guests, Linda Garcia, a renowned figure in public service, will be gracing the occasion. Known for her tireless advocacy for education reform and community development, Garcia's presence is sure to add a touch of inspiration and expertise to the event.

Another notable attendee is "The Author", a teenage wordsmith whose literary works have captivated readers worldwide. It is rumored that The Author is considering a run for public office soon.

The event promises to be an exceptional opportunity for networking, sharing ideas, and fostering collaboration among esteemed individuals in public service.
As the evening unfolds, it is expected that this gathering will set the stage for meaningful collaborations, inspiring future endeavors, and laying the groundwork for positive change within our community.

Stay tuned for more updates on this event as it progresses, as our team will be reporting on the highlights and key discussions that emerge throughout the night."

*Randy hit the jackpot!*

*Randy: "HOLY SHIT! MS. GARCIA AND THE AUTHOR!? THIS TELLS ME EXACTLY WHERE THEY ARE BOTH GOING TO BE TONIGHT!"*

*He started to kiss the newspaper out of joy. He stood up tall and his confidence came back!*

36

*Randy: "This newspaper is such a blessing! I'll be able to save the future now!"*

*So, he planned to show up and confront them tonight, for the sake of the world.*

*******************************************************************

*The Author was putting on his best suit in his room. He had an all-black suit, with a red shirt and a black tie. He thought it was a good fit that matched his personality. He looked in the mirror and felt amazing. Then his phone began to ring.*

*Author: "Wow everybody keeps calling me today!"*

*He looked at his phone and it was his buddy Damaris calling him. Damaris is a chill dude, The Author and him became friends in their freshman year of high school and they've been close since. He answered the phone.*

*Author: "Yo!"*

*Damaris: "Hey Author, what's good man?"*

*Author: "Not much, I'm just getting ready to go to this event."*

*Damaris: "Oh yeah, it said that you were attending an event in the newspaper today."*

*Author: "It did? I thought Linda was just bluffing about that."*

*Damaris: "Yeah Short Kid told me, I'm a normal 18-year-old boy, I don't read the newspaper, cause that's lame, Haha."*

*Author: "Oh."*

*Damaris: "I was going to ask if you wanted to go fishing with me and my cousin Jared, but I know you can't."*

*Author: "Well first, you don't have to specify that Jared is your cousin, I already know that. Secondly bro, I do apologize, but let's say we hang out Wednesday with The Short Kid?"*

*Damaris: "Bet bro."*

*Author: "Bet, see you then."*

*They ended the call and Author began to brush his teeth with bubblegum toothpaste. A few minutes later, Natasha came to his house. She was wearing a beautiful dress, and she surprised The Author when she walked in.*

*Author: "Oh, that's a really nice dress!"*

*Natasha blushed at his comment. They were in his room finishing up getting ready.*

*Natasha: "Big A, I'm going downstairs to wait for our ride, I will meet you down there."*

*Author: "Okay, I'll be right down."*

*She headed downstairs, and The Author was gathering all his belongings. He was looking for his wallet and he could not recall where he had left it.*

*Author: "Where is my wallet? Maybe it's on my bed somewhere?"*

*He looked all over his bed, and he couldn't find it. He lifted up his pillowcase and while his wallet was not there, that vape The Short Kid gave him was sitting right there. He picked it up, and looked at it for a second, then put it in the inside pocket of his blazer.*

*Natasha: "AYE! OUR DRIVER IS HERE!"*

*Author: "OKAY I'LL BE RIGHT THERE!"*

*Natasha: "HEY IS IT COOL IF I KEEP THIS JAR OF PEANUT BUTTER I FOUND IN YOUR KITCHEN?"*

*Author: "UH, YEAH, SURE?"*

*The Author ran down the stairs. They left his crib and got in the car. They were officially headed off to the event! They didn't know what to expect once they arrived and they were both slightly anxious. Natasha's stomach began to make rumbling noises.*

*Natasha: "Sorry, when I get nervous my stomach makes noises."*

*Author: "It's all good."*

*When they finally arrived at the banquet hall, the two of them walked inside. When they got into the building, it was absolutely beautiful! The walls were gold plated, there were shiny chandeliers, and even a fucking chocolate fountain!*

*Author: "I love it here!"*

*He looked at Nat's face, and she seemed like she was in paradise! From a far, The Author heard someone call out his name, He looked over fast because he thought he was getting pulled up on, but he saw it was just Ms. Garcia! She ran over to greet them.*

*Ms. Garcia: "Author! It's so good to see you!"*

*Author: "Hi! It's so good to see you too!"*

*Ms. Garcia: "Who's your friend?"*

*Natasha: "Hi, I'm Natasha. I believe we met last year."*

*Ms. Garcia: "Oh yeah I remember, at the carnival, right?"*

*Natasha: "Haha, yeah."*

*Author: "Those were crazy times."*

*They all chuckled like they were snobby rich people.*

*Ms. Garcia: "Well Author, there is a lot of people here who would like to meet you."*

*He thought to himself "Who the hell wants to meet with me?"*

*Author: "Sounds great, we'll be right there!"*

*Ms. Garcia: "Great! I'll meet you in the other room!"*

*She walked away and started talking with some other guest. Suddenly, The Author started to have anxiety out of nowhere. He felt like his breathing got heavier, and his hands were getting sweaty.*

*Author: "Hey Nat, I'll be right back I'm going to the bathroom!"*

*Natasha: "Okay, is everything alright?"*

*Author: "Yeah, I'm good, it's just a man thing, you know, you like wouldn't understand."*

*He ran to the bathroom because he needed to compose himself and prepare to meet and talk to all these self-proclaimed powerful people. Once he got to the bathroom, he looked in the mirror and took a deep breath.*

*Author: "I would do anything to just relax a bit, I think I had too much coffee today!"*

*That's when he remembered that there was a vape in his pocket. He took it out of his jacket pocket and held it gently in the palm of his hand. He contemplated if he should hit it. He looked at himself in the mirror and took a deep breath in to process everything.*

*Author: "Well, sure, might as well have a fun night!"*

*He turned the vape on, put it near his lips, and pressed the button that let out all the smoke. He inhaled it in and slowly blew it all out. After that his anxiety had gone away, and he felt tremendously better.*

*Author: "Yum!"*

*So, he decided to take another hit. He put it up to his mouth and took a 20 second hit of the vape pen. But, as he was hitting the vape, some older man in a 3-piece suit walked into the bathroom and saw exactly what he was doing! But The Author didn't really care that much, he just assumed that dude in a suit was just another guest at the event. He gave The Author a dirty look as he was putting the vape back in his pocket. But Author didn't give a shit. He walked out of the bathroom feeling refreshed and prepared himself to fake smile the rest of the night. He went to the main room and met up with Nat.*

*Natasha: "Hey, where have you been?"*

*Author: "The gentleman's room, that's what it was labeled as on the door."*

*Natasha: "Oh ok, I'm glad you're here because the senators or whatever are supposed to make a few speeches soon!"*

*Author: "Great, I came back just in time to get bored."*

*There was a big stage where all the politicians were going to speak at. He grabbed Nat's hand and guided themselves to the very front of the stage.*

*Natasha: "You became such a gentleman after going to that bathroom."*

*After a few minutes, Ms. Garcia went on the stage and started to speak into the microphone.*

*Ms. Garcia: "Good evening, everybody! It's great to have you all here with us, I am very honored to be up here and introduce a few of our great state senators and local representatives!"*

*The entire crowd was clapping, so far, The Author was having a good time!*

*Ms. Garcia: "And now... I would like to invite onto the stage... OUR GREAT ELECTED OFFICIALS!"*

*Everybody started to clap, and the elected officials began to walk across stage doing their dramatic entrances. One by one they walked on stage and The Author and Nat were clapping for each one of them.*

*Ms. Garcia: "Finally to save the best for last, I would like to introduce you all to Senator Meatball!"*

*Then one more man walked on stage, and he was wearing a 3-piece suit...*

*Natasha: "Isn't this great Author?"*

*Author: "Oh my god..."*

*The guy who caught The Author vaping in the bathroom was a senator! The second he laid his eyes on The Author he looked disgusted with him. Author felt so embarrassed! He didn't want to tell Nat or Ms. Garcia about what happened, he was just too ashamed... After a bit The Author had just finished talking with all the politicians who all had the fakest personalities, and he decided to get some drinks at the bar. He got tipsy off this drink called a Kitty Cocktail, which is a mixture of lemon lime soda and red syrup.*

*Author: "BARTENDER!"*

*Author: "Let me get another drink over here!"*

*Natasha: "A, I think you've had enough."*

*Author: "Listen... I'll tell you when I've had enough!"*

*Natasha: "Stop acting drunk, you are literally drinking a nonalcoholic kiddie drink!"*

*He laid his head down on the bar counter. Suddenly he felt a hand on his shoulder. He picked his head up feeling dazed, and turned around, it was Ms. Garcia.*

*Ms. Garcia: "Author, someone would like to speak with you!"*

*Author: "Please don't tell me it's a senator."*

*Ms. Garcia: "No better, he is a local millionaire, and he really wants to talk to you!"*

*Author: "Really? That's odd, what's his name?"*

*Ms. Garcia: "His name is Mr. Theodore."*

*Author: "Alright then, I'll go talk with him."*

*So, he got up and she walked him into a private area to speak with this guy. Nat decided that she would just wait at the bar. Once they arrived in the private section, she introduced The Author to the man.*

*Ms. Garcia: "Mr. Theodore, this is The Author"*

*He stood up and they shook hands.*

*Mr. Theodore: "The infamous teenage writer, it's so good to finally meet you!"*

*Ms. Garcia: "I'll walk away to let you two chat."*

*She left the area, and it was just The Author and this guy sitting there alone. He was an older man, and he was wearing a trench coat and held a purple cane.*

*Author: "Hi sir?"*

*The Author was super confused, he had no clue who this guy was. For a second, he thought this dude was a pimp!*

*Mr. Theodore: "My grandson Murphy has told me so many great things about you!"*

*The Author thought to himself "Holy guacamole! It's Murphy's super rich grandpa!"*

*Author: "Hi! I've heard so many great things about you sir!"*

*Mr. Theodore: "Haha, I'm assuming Murphy has told you about me?"*

*Author: "Yeah, all the time! He looks up to you!"*

*Mr. Theodore: "That's so nice to hear!"*

*They talked for a while. He genuinely was a super nice man. He told Author about how he's been running hundreds of homeless shelters and orphanages all over their state for over 20 years now! The best part of his story was that he does it out of the kindness in his heart. He said he doesn't make any profit doing any of this.*

*Author: "Wow Mr. Theodore, that's truly amazing!"*

*Mr. Theodore: "Thank you!"*

*Mr. Theodore: "Listen, how about sometime you stop by our one shelter right here in town, it's the biggest one I own, and I could give you and some friends a look around?"*

*Author: "Definitely, I will make it a priority! Does tomorrow work for you?"*

*Mr. Theodore: "Yes! Is around noon good?"*

*Author: "Yes, I'll see you then!"*

*They shook hands and he told The Author he would be heading out for the night. Mr. Theodore left the banquet hall and The Author walked back to the bar.*

*Natasha: "Bartender can I get another drink?"*

*"Listen kid, I could get into a lot of trouble for giving you that Margarita earlier, no more for you, okay?"*

*Natasha: "OH screw you pal!"*

*The Author: "Everything alright over here?"*

*Natasha: "Yeah, I think I'm ready to call it a night Author."*

*Author: "Same, let me just say goodbye to Ms. Garcia."*

*So, they walked over to Ms. Garcia and told her that they were going to be heading out, she thanked them for coming and she gave them both a hug.*

*Author: "Hey Ms. G, quickly before I leave, I wanted to ask you if tomorrow at noon can you meet me at the big shelter in town, Mr. Theodore wanted me to visit and bring some people to show us around?"*

*Ms. Garcia: "Well yes I can come..."*

*Author: "GREAT see you then!"*

*Ms. Garcia: "But don't you have school?"*

*Author: "Oh don't even worry about it."*

*******************************************************************

*Meanwhile, Randy was right outside the banquet hall...*

*Randy: "Alright this is the place."*

*He walked closer up to the doors and gave himself a quick pep talk.*

*Randy: "Ok, I'll go in there and warn everyone about Murphy, I'll find The Author and Ms. Garcia and have them come with me!"*

*He took a deep breath, and bursted open the doors!*

*Randy: "EVERYONE I NEED YOUR ATTENTION!"*

*The whole room gasped! He ran through the entire building screaming!*

*Senator Meatball: "Who is this idiot!?"*

*Randy: "THIS IS IMPORTANT WE NEED TO STOP HIM NOW!"*

*Author: "What the hell?"*

*Randy turned around when he heard The Author say that.*

*Randy: "Oh my gosh, it's you! I came here to find you!"*

*Author: "What the yuck are you talking about dude?"*

*Natasha: "This guy weird as hell."*

*He turned his head and switched his attention over when he saw his friend, Ms. Garcia. However, this version of her is not the same person he once knew.*

*Randy: "Oh my gosh, Linda, it is... so great you are alive!"*

*He slowly walked towards her.*

*Ms. Garcia "You better back up."*

*Randy: "Listen, you both have to come with me, we need to stop Murphy-!"*

*She gave him a right hook and knocked him out!*

*Author: "Woah! That was sick!"*

*The police came running over to Randy and 3 of them jumped on him! They then began to tase him!*

*Randy: "AHHHHH!"*

*The police aggressively pulled him up and put handcuffs on him!*

*"You are under arrest!"*

*Randy: "SERIOUSLY!? YA'LL REALLY PUTTING CHARGES ON ME RIGHT NOW?!"*

*The cops dragged him out of the banquet hall.*

*Randy: "YOU ARE MAKING A MISTAKE!"*

*One of the cops hit him with the taser again and he passed out. They dragged him out the doors and everyone in the banquet hall was told to leave immediately.*

*Author: "Damn Linda! I wasn't expecting you to take that creep out like that!"*

*Ms. Garcia: "My mamma always taught me to be a fighter!"*

*Natasha: "What was that all about?"*

*Author: "I have no idea, but that was weird..."*

*Ms. Garcia: "Why did he come specifically to you and me?"*

*The two of them were so confused by what had just occurred.*

*Author: "Am I tripping but was that dude wearing... a jetpack?"*

*Natasha: "Those don't really exist."*

*Author: "True."*

*The cops began pushing everybody out the building. All the politicians were escorted out of the building safely. The three friends went outside and resumed talking.*

*Author: "I'm just so confused, and a little shaken up."*

*Ms. Garcia: "Listen, let's all just go home and get some rest."*

*Natasha: "That sounds like a good idea, come on Author."*

*Author: "Alright, peace out Ms. G."*

*Ms. Garcia: "I'll see you tomorrow."*

*Ms. Garcia went to her car, confused by what just occurred.*

*Ms. Garcia: "What the hell was that all about?"*

*Natasha and The Author's personal driver pulled up and they both hopped in the backseat.*

*Author: "Hey man, thanks for driving us all over today."*

*The young man driving the SUV wearing sunglasses responded in a chill tone "No problem bro."*

*Author: "I enjoy cruising with you, is it alright if I call you The Cruiser?"*

*Natasha began to chuckle.*

*The Cruiser: "Yeah man I fuck with that name!"*

*Author: "Your cool, wanna hit this vape?"*

*The Cruiser: "Yes please!"*

*The Author started to tell them both about what happened in the bathroom with the senator, and Natasha thought it was hilarious!*

*Natasha: "You are the only kid in the entire world who gets caught vaping by a senator!"*

*Her and The Cruiser were laughing hysterically. The Author was at least glad they could get a laugh out of his embarrassing moment.*

*Author: "Yeah, I just think that dude at the end was creepy and killed the vibe."*

*Natasha: "Yeah it was so strange, but whatever the cops got him."*

*The Author felt like there was more to it than just he some random crazy guy.*

*Author: "Did I mishear him, because it sounded like he said something about Murphy or something?"*

*Natasha: "No I'm pretty sure he said, um, we need Mercury, or something like that."*

*Author: "That doesn't even make any sense."*

*Natasha: "That's the thing, crazy people don't make sense!"*

*Author: "You know what, that's so true…"*

*It was 2:55 AM and Randy had been thrown in a cell at the local police station!*

*Randy: "LET ME THE HELL OUT OF HERE!"*

*One of the cops looked at him and screamed at him!*

*"Shut your damn mouth!"*

*Randy: "PLEASE! YOU ARE MAKING A MISTAKE!"*

*The cop responded to him.*

*"I TOLD YOU TO SHUT YOUR FUCKING MOUTH!"*

*Meanwhile, in the investigation room, a detective and one of the police officers who arrested Randy were talking...*

*Officer Coleslaw: "He caused a huge disturbance at the banquet hall, and he harassed many of the guests at the event."*

*Detective Gadget: "What type of event was this?"*

*Officer Coleslaw: "Some political thing."*

*Detective Gadget: "Oh so he's just one of those extremists huh? Figures."*

*Officer Coleslaw: "We searched him, he has no ID, he had some sort of weapon that looked like a toy gun, and, it appears he has some sort of fancy backpack."*

*Detective Gadget: "Odd, but whatever, keep him here for the week, we'll transfer him to another jail over the weekend."*

*Officer Coleslaw: "Got it."*

*Detective Gadget: "And keep his items in the evidence room, I'd like to further inspect them."*

*The cop agreed and he went to his walkie talkie and spoke to the one officer near the holding cells.*

*Officer Coleslaw: "Officer, please let the suspect know he won't be getting out of here anytime soon."*

*Randy heard him say that over the cop's walkie! He had a frightened look on his face! The cop next to him smiled and laughed!*

*"You heard him, so get comfortable buddy!"*

*He then left the room.*

*Randy: "PLEASE LET ME OUT BEFORE IT'S TO LATE, MURPHY WILL KILL US ALL!"*

*The cop left the room, and nobody was around to hear him. Randy sat down in his cell and put his head down.*

*Randy: "Barging into the banquet hall like that was the worst mistake of my life."*

*He stood up and stared out the tiny window in his cell and looked out at the moon.*

*Randy: "I failed my mission. I've failed them all…"*

*\*\*\*\*\*\*\*\*\*\*\*\*\*\*\*\*\*\*\*\*\*\*\*\*\*\*\*\*\*\*\*\*\*\*\*\*\*\*\*\*\*\*\*\*\*\*\*\*\*\*\*\*\*\*\*\*\*\*\*\*\*\*\*\*\*\*\*\*\*\*\**

*The Author walked into his first class of the day and saw The Short Kid sitting in the back of the class, hitting his vape like he usually does.*

*Author: "Bro really in class?"*

*Short Kid: "It's ok bro, the teacher isn't here."*

*This was typical of him, so Author wasn't even surprised.*

*Short Kid: "So how was the event buddy?"*

*Author: "Oh my gosh, well first that vape…"*

*Short Kid: "What about it?"*

*Author: "Actually, never mind, it was fine, but some crazy guy towards the end of the night really messed everything up."*

*Short Kid: "Holy shit, everything good?"*

*Author: "Yeah, I'm just going to ignore it because I want to focus on our graduation stuff till Saturday."*

*Short Kid: "Yeah, don't even worry about it, he's probably just another political extremist."*

*Author: "True."*

*The Author sat down in his desk, and put his head down, until he heard someone talk to him.*

*"Sup man?"*

*Author: "I swear this better be important."*

*He looked up, and it was his one friend Marcus.*

*Marcus: "What up boy?"*

*Marcus and him had been friends for a few years at this point. Marcus is this extremely buff dude, who wears the same thing every day to school, a white tank top and blue jeans. He enjoyed showing off his big ass arms. Even in the cold weather he'd only wear the white tank top. He told everyone that his muscle was all natural, but one time a few months prior, The Author walked into the gym locker room and saw him inject himself with a needle filled with steroid. Anyway, back in class...*

*Marcus: "I hate school man! I wish I was pumping up at the gym right now!"*

*Short Kid: "What's with you always talking about the motherfuckin' gym?"*

*Marcus: "Listen midget, you wouldn't understand, but the grind never stops."*

*Marcus sat down at the desk right next to The Author. Marcus is overly aggressive with everything he does, so when he sat down, he shook the entire classroom and slammed his big beefy arms onto the desk! He made so much noise and everyone in the class was staring at him.*

*Marcus: "What are you all looking at?"*

*He then started to flex his biceps and showed them off to the entire classroom.*

*Marcus: "You're all staring because you wish you had these babies on your pathetic little arms."*

*Short Kid: "NO! We're all looking you cause you are acting like a fucking dumbass!"*

*The Author started to get secondhand embarrassment from this entire situation. Marcus and The Short Kid started talking shit to each other, when the teacher walked in the classroom.*

*Author: "Oh great, Mr. Bill is here."*

*This teacher and him were not on good terms the entire school year. When he found out about The Author's books, he became enraged by The Author's use of foul language in his writing. When Mr. Bill sat at his desk The Short Kid said something under his breath...*

*Short Kid: "He looks like a hillbilly."*

*The whole class began to chuckle, and everyone was trying to hold back their laughter! Mr. Bill then started to drink a diet soda. He would always refer to it as a healthy alternative to water.*

*Marcus looked over at The Author and said something quietly in his ear.*

*Marcus: "That dude needs to hit the gym."*

*The Author was holding in so much laughter!*

*Mr. Bill: "Class can you settle down please! I know you all hate me, and I hate you all too! I'm retiring in a few days, and I can't wait to get my sweet pension and never have to see you bastards ever again!"*

*He took a sip of his diet soda and felt like a badass.*

*Mr. Bill: "Anyway, since it's one of our last days of school, I thought I'd make it simple and read a book to you little assholes!"*

*The Author started to zone out.*

*Mr. Bill: "I will be reading a book called War and Peace."*

*Marcus: "UGH! BORING!"*

*Mr. Bill: "Hey shut the fuck up back there and pay attention!"*

*The Author was super annoyed already. He had planned to sneak out of school before noon to meet up with Murphy's grandfather at the shelter. So, at that moment The Author decided he had enough for the day. He stood up and headed for the door.*

*Mr. Bill: "AUTHOR! WHERE THE FUCK DO YOU THINK YOU ARE GOING?!"*

*Author: "Listen dude…"*

*Mr. Bill: "DON'T TALK BACK TO ME!"*

*Author: "Ight, I'm going to head out."*

*He walked out the door in a dash and the teacher screamed at him!*

*Mr. Bill: "By the way, Principal Martinez has been looking for you, don't think just because your graduating in a few days doesn't mean your immune to consequences!"*

*The Author heard him and ignored everything he said. He decided that he was going to sneak out of school a little bit earlier than he had originally planned.*

*Author: "Okay, I need to avoid any faculty, especially the hall monitors!"*

*He snuck through the second floor avoiding everybody in sight. He got to the staircase and slowly walked down each step. He walked through the first floor of the school and headed on over to the unlocked door by the cafeteria. He slowly walked over to the door when he heard from behind him someone's keys shaking. The Author felt like a deer in headlights. He thought to himself "Oh shoot, it's Martinez."*

*Principal Martinez: "Author… I've been looking for you."*

*He turned around and they made direct eye contact.*

*Author: "Hey PrinciPAL, emphasis on pal because you are my pal, what's up?"*

*Principal Martinez: "What's up is that you have 40 truancies, and 15 tardy's for the past two weeks, all unexcused."*

*Author: "I think there might be an error in your system because I've been here every day."*

*The door was right next to them, he had almost made it out of the school. "Shit!" The Author thought to himself.*

*Principal Martinez: "Come with me to the office now."*

*The Author took a deep breath and looked at the principal.*

*Author: "That's not going to happen."*

*He then booked it to the door and ran out of the school as fast as he could!*

*Author: "See you later alligator!"*

*Principal Martinez: "This isn't over Author! I'll see you in detention tomorrow!"*

*The Author ran as fast as he could until he made it off campus. His heart was beating fast, and he felt super thrilled!*

*Author: "That was amazing!"*

*He checked his phone and it was only 9:30 AM.*

*Author: "Damn, I got almost three hours to kill."*

*So, he decided to walk on over to the coffee shop and drink a few cups of coffee to pass the time. At around 11:00, Riley called The Author, and he picked it up right away!*

*Author: "Hey babe!"*

*Riley: "Author, Short Kid told me that you left school again! And people are saying Martinez chased you out of the school and you threw dirt at him!"*

*Author: "Okay that's like 75% true, but who the hell said I threw dirt at him?"*

*Riley: "Author listen to me, you are going to get into so much trouble for this! Where are you now?"*

*Author: "Just at the coffee shop."*

*Riley: "Oh Author..."*

*Author: "I'm so quirky I know."*

*Riley: "Are you coming back?"*

*Author: "No, remember when we talked last night, I told you I was going to meet up with that millionaire dude."*

*Riley: "Okay you know what babe…"*

*Author: "What!"*

*Riley: "I am coming with you! I want to spend more time with you."*

*Author: "Aw really?! But wait, how are you going to get out of school?"*

*Riley: "I'll figure out a way."*

*The Author wanted her to come, and they tried to figure out a way to get her out of school.*

*Riley: "I'll just run out the door like you did."*

*Author: "No, you'll be in trouble like me…"*

*Riley: "Damn I don't know then."*

*Author: "WAIT! I have an idea."*

*He told her his idea, and she loved it, so then they decided to execute it…. The phone in the attendance office began to ring and the secretary in the office answered it.*

*"Yes hello?"*

*It was The Author calling, and he put on a fake deep voice...*

*Author: "Hello Ma'am, this is Riley's father calling, I'd like to excuse her from school for the rest of the day."*

*"Certainly, no problem, what is the reasoning for her being excused?"*

*Author: "Um."*

*He had to think fast.*

*Author: "Her... mother... is... in the hospital."*

*"Oh my, okay, we'll call her down and send her a pass to leave campus right away."*

*Author: "Thank you so much."*

*He hung up the phone, and Riley was called down to the office and the secretary wrote her a pass to leave.*

*"Your mother is in my prayers."*

*Riley: "Thank you?"*

*She wrote her the pass, and she left the school and walked over to the coffee shop The Author was at. She walked through the door and the couple ran up to each other and hugged!*

*Author: "Hey you made it!"*

*Riley: "Yeah! Just curious, but what did you tell the attendance lady?"*

*Author: "Oh, nothing really."*

*He pulled out his phone to check the time.*

*Author: "It's 11:45, we should head over there now."*

*So, he decided to call for a ride. The night before he took down The Cruiser's contact information, and he decided to give him a call and ask for a ride again. He told Author he'd pick him up right away! Only a few minutes later, he rolled up to the coffee shop and the two of them hopped in the back.*

*The Cruiser: "Yo, good to see you again today, Author."*

*Author: "Hey man good to see you again today, this is my girl, Riley."*

*Riley: "Hello."*

*The Cruiser: "Yo, I thought that girl from yesterday was your girlfriend?"*

*Author: "Haha, no, just a friend."*

*Riley: "Yeah, she better be just a friend."*

*They all laughed, and after a 10-minute car ride he dropped them off in front of the big building. They hopped out of the whip and walked up to the entrance. Once they walked in, they were intrigued by what they saw.*

*Riley: "This place is huge!"*

*They took a few steps in, and the building was packed with people! The Author felt a hand on his shoulder and was spooked!*

*Author: "ZOINKS!"*

*He turned around and it was just Ms. Garcia.*

*Ms. Garcia: "Woah, didn't mean to scare you!"*

*Author: "it's all good, I've just been feeling a bit jumpy after what happened last night."*

*Ms. Garcia: "Before we go see Mr. Theodore, I wanted to show you what was in the paper today."*

*Author: "Oh boy."*

*She handed him the newspaper and he began to read it...*

*Unidentified Man Arrested for Harassment*

"In a shocking turn of events at last night's highly anticipated political gathering held at the prestigious banquet hall, an unidentified man was taken into custody for harassing guests.

The event, attended by prominent political figures and community members, was disrupted when an individual began harassing guests. Eyewitnesses reported that the man was behaving aggressively and creating a disturbance, causing distress among attendees. Law-enforcement swiftly intervened, apprehending the suspect and ensuring the safety of all present.

Local authorities commended the swift response of the officers in attendance and expressed their commitment to maintaining a safe environment at public events. They are currently investigating the motives behind the unidentified man's actions and will take necessary legal actions to address the harassment incident..."

*The Author threw the paper down on the ground.*

*Author: "Whatever that's stupid."*

*Riley: "Don't even worry about it."*

*Ms. Garcia: "Yeah let's just meet with Mr. T."*

*Riley: "Okay let me just finish sending this text to my chiropractor first."*

*Ms. Garcia began walking them towards the back of the building where Mr. Theodore's office was at. As they walked past, they saw what appeared to be almost 100 people living there, eating food provided by the staff, being given new clothes, and were being provided the necessary resources to survive. They each even had their own nice beds to sleep on.*

*Author: "Wow, that's truly admirable."*

*The Author truly loved what he was seeing. They approached the door to Mr. Theodore's office and Ms. Garcia knocked on it.*

*Mr. Theodore: "Come on in!"*

*She opened the door and they all walked in the office. Mr. Theodore was sitting at his desk and stood up to greet them.*

*Mr. Theodore: "Linda and The Author, it's so good to see you both."*

*They both shook his hand. Then Mr. Theodore looked over at Riley.*

*Mr. Theodore: "And I assume you must be Ms. Author?"*

*Riley laughed at that.*

*Riley: "I've never had anyone call me that, but I love it!"*

*Author: "Do you really?"*

*Riley: "Yeah!"*

*The Author blushed.*

*Mr. Theodore: "Okay you two love birds, I would be thrilled to give you a tour!"*

*Author: "Sounds great!"*

*As they were about to walk out of his office, Mr. Theodore's secretary stepped in and said something to him.*

*"Sir, you haven't picked up your heart medication in 3 weeks."*

*Mr. Theodore: "Not a big deal, I'll just get it later.*

*She then left the room.*

*Mr. Theodore: "Alright let's do this!"*

*They all walked out of the room, and he began the tour. Mr. Theodore first took them to the kitchen.*

*Mr. Theodore: "This here is our kitchen, where we make the food for all of our guests."*

*Riley: "That's so sweet you call them guest."*

*Mr. Theodore: "Well of course! I consider the people we provide for here as our guests."*

*The chef was in the kitchen preparing lunch for everybody in the building. Ms. Garcia was offered a ladle full of soup just prepared by the chef. She took a sip of it and said it was amazing!*

*Mr. Theodore: "I like to provide my guest with the best food out there."*

*The Author was surprised. He thought in most places like this, the homeless people were given the most disgusting food. He was pleasantly surprised* to not see a single tuna sandwich being passed out. Mr. Theodore walked them out of the kitchen and took them to the main hallway that they had already walked through.

Mr. Theodore: "You had to walk through this area already, so I won't talk about it for that long, but this is where all of our guests stay."

Riley: "Cool!"

Mr. Theodore: "Now I know this tour just began, but do any of you have questions?"

The Author: "Sir, this is more of a comment, but what you are doing here is really amazing!"

Mr. Theodore: "Thank you for that, I appreciate your compliment."

The Author: "I just have to ask, what makes you want to do all this? You don't make any profit, right?"

Mr. Theodore: "I don't make a penny off any of this. Once I became a millionaire, I realize that I had to give back to people, and honestly doing this brings me happiness."

Riley: "Do you have any other locations?"

Mr. Theodore: "I do, I own homeless shelters all over the state, and I own a few orphanages in the city. And just like this location I don't make any *money in return. The only thing I get in return is the bright smiles from the people I help."*

*Riley noticed a single mother with two children sitting on one of the beds nearby. Mr. Theodore saw her looking over.*

*Mr. Theodore: "That over there is Gwen and her two boys, her baby daddy threw her out, and they came here one rainy night, and ever since then she's been staying here trying to get back up on her feet."*

*She was feeding her boys the freshly prepared soup. The Author was fascinated that Murphy's grandfather was such a good man. The Author has always wanted to help people, even though he doesn't always make the right decisions. He truly admired what Mr. Theodore was doing here and at all the other locations. He was glad to be best friends with his grandson.*

*Mr. Theodore: "People assume all of us rich guys are egotistical, power-hungry, pieces of crap! To be honest, for the most part, it is true. But I wanna break that cycle, I want to change people's perception. I've been very fortunate in my life, and I have the ability to help people. I literally own a skyscraper in the city with my name on it, so doing all of this clearly isn't a burden on my finances!*

*Author: "That's true."*

*Mr. Theodore: "I know one day my grandson Murphy will keep my legacy going and will continue to help people just like me."*

*The three of them were in awe of Mr. Theodore's generosity.*

*Mr. Theodore: "Do any of you have more questions?"*

*The Author: "No, but I'd like to see more of this big ass place!"*

*Mr. Theodore laughed.*

*Mr. Theodore: "Well all right then! Let's continue..."*

*He froze for a moment and didn't say a word. At first the gang just thought he was taking a pause to collect his thoughts or something. But then they realized something was off.*

*Author: "Sir, are you okay?"*

*He wasn't saying a word, and he began to intensely sweat. He started to breathe super heavily, and he fell to his knees. He put his hand over his chest and his face began to turn red!*

*Ms. Garcia: "I THINK HE IS HAVING A HEART ATTACK!"*

*The Author remembered the secretary told Mr. Theodore about his heart medication!*

*Author: "Oh no..."*

*Then all the guests in the shelter were looking over and were starting to get concerned!*

*Author: "We need to call an ambulance now!"*

*Riley took out her phone and dialed 911. His breathing kept getting heavier and heavier, and he eventually became unconscious...*

■■■■■■■■■■■■■■■■■■■■■■■■■■■■■■■■■■■■■■■■■■■■■■■

*In the police station, one of the cops threw the newspaper in Randy's cell.*

*"Check it out, you made the front page."*

*Randy picked it up and read the story.*

*Randy: "God damn it!"*

*"I have great news for you!"*

*Randy got excited!*

*"You won't be staying here much longer!"*

*Randy thought to himself "FINALLY! Now I can get back out there and stop Murphy!" until the cop said...*

*"You'll be transferred tomorrow to a high security prison with some of the world's most deadly criminals! You messed with the wrong people last night bud."*

*The cop walked away laughing.*

*Randy: "FUCK! I need to get out of here, NOW!"*

*Randy didn't know what else to do, so then, he came up with a plan.*

*Randy: "Fuck this, I'm breaking out of this rat-infested place tomorrow!"*

*******************************************************************

*The Author was sitting in the hospital waiting room with Riley and Ms. Garcia when Murphy arrived!*

*Murphy: "WHAT'S GOING ON?!"*

*The Author stood up.*

*Author: "Your grandpa had a heart attack. It's not looking good right now."*

*A doctor came out of the room and approached all of them.*

*Murphy: "Doc, is my grandpa going to be okay."*

*The doctor had a sad look on his face.*

*"Your grandfather went into cardiac arrest. We did everything we could... I'm sorry, but we lost him..."*

*Murphy's heart sank as he received the devastating news. He couldn't comprehend that his beloved grandfather would be gone forever.*

*Murphy: "Oh my god, no..."*

*Author: "I'm so sorry Murphy."*

*The Author stood up and gave his friend a hug.*

*Author: "He loved you so much."*

*Riley and Ms. Garcia began to tear up as this moment unfolded. Riley stood up and comforted Murphy.*

*Riley: "I am so sorry for your loss."*

*Ms. Garcia stood up too.*

*Ms. Garcia: "He was a great man."*

*The three of them stood around Murphy and they all shared a group hug... Then after about 5 minutes of grieving in the hospital lobby, a man with a briefcase walked into the hospital and approached Murphy.*

*"Hi Murphy, I'd like to give you my deepest condolences for your loss. I was your grandfather's estate lawyer, could you possibly come to my office in about 20 minutes? I need to talk to you. My office is right down the street from here."*

*Murphy: "Sure, uh, I'll meet you there."*

*The lawyer then walked away. Then Murphy looked over at The Author.*

*Murphy: "Man, would you be able to come with me?"*

*Author: "Of course, I'll be there to support you."*

*He looked over at Riley.*

*Author: "Hey babe, I need to go with him somewhere, do you have a way home?"*

*Ms. Garcia chimed in.*

*Ms. Garcia: "I'll take her home, just focus on being a good friend right now."*

*Riley grabbed The Author's hand.*

*Riley: "I will be good, I love you."*

*Author: "I love you too."*

*She let go of his hand, and The Author and Murphy walked down the street to the lawyer's office...*

*******************************************************************

*Meanwhile, Damaris and The Short Kid were hanging out after school ended. They were at Damaris's house watching TV.*

*Short Kid: "Dude, and he just walked out the classroom!"*

*Damaris: "What the hell, where did he go?"*

*Short Kid: "I have no idea!"*

*The breaking news logo appeared on the news.*

*"Good afternoon, we have a breaking story just coming in..."*

*Short Kid: "Oh shit."*

*"An armed bank robbery has been prevented by the vigilante known as The PyroManiac! The hero was seen fighting off the robbers, using brutal force. Distorted camera footage shows him fleeing from the scene, no bystanders were injured."*

*The two of them paid close attention.*

*Damaris: "Dude, can you believe there is an actual superhero out there?!"*

*Short Kid: "It's fucking crazy, I've heard rumors that PyroManiac can take on bullets!"*

*Damaris: "I've heard that he wears this cool ass gas mask everywhere he goes!"*

*Short Kid: "I bet if we lived in the city, we would see him all the time!"*

*Damaris: "Maybe bro."*

*Damaris's dad came into the living room.*

*"Mijo, take out the trash."*

*Damaris stood up and took the garbage outside when suddenly Short Kid got a call from Riley. He then answered the phone.*

*Short Kid: "Yo, what's good?"*

*Riley: "Short Kid, something tragic has happened..."*

*He sat there while she told him what had just occurred.*

*Short Kid: "What..."*

\*\*\*\*\*\*\*\*\*\*\*\*\*\*\*\*\*\*\*\*\*\*\*\*\*\*\*\*\*\*\*\*\*\*\*\*\*\*\*\*\*\*\*\*\*\*\*\*\*\*\*\*\*\*\*\*\*\*\*\*\*\*\*\*\*\*\*\*

*The Author and Murphy were sitting in the lawyer's office when he began speaking directly to Murphy.*

*"As you know, your grandfather was an incredibly wealthy man."*

*Murphy: "Yes?"*

*"Well, he wrote a will, and I'd like to read it to you."*

*Murphy: "Alright."*

*"He wrote 'My dearest grandson, after much consideration, and pushback from my advisors, I have decided that even after my passing, I would like all my operations to continue running. I am proud for you to be informed that I am leaving you everything that I have...' Hold on let me flip to the next page."*

*Murphy and The Author were both stunned!*

*Murphy: "Did you just say everything?!"*

*"Let me finish, he goes on to say 'I am leaving you with my million-dollar fortune. I am also leaving you my skyscraper, the shelters I own and the orphanages in the city. You shall receive all of this effective immediately. I know you will keep my legacy strong. I love you.' So yeah, it's pretty clear what he has left you..."*

*Murphy: "Oh my fucking... this can't be real!"*

*Author: "Murphy, do you realize what this means?!"*

*Murphy: "I-."*

*Author: "You're a millionaire..."*

*Murphy: "Oh my god!"*

*The lawyer handed him the briefcase with everything he needed inside.*

*"Congratulations Murphy."*

*They left the lawyer's office in complete shock.*

*Murphy: "I can't believe this is happening..."*

*Author: "This is insane bro!"*

*Murphy: "I don't even know what to think right now."*

*Author: "Dude you are super fucking rich now!"*

*Murphy: "I can't believe he left it all to me!"*

*Author: "Remember bro, be responsible with the money and remember to process his passing first, then keep his legacy strong."*

*Murphy: "I said yesterday I always wanted to be like him and now... I have that opportunity. I will be better than him in every single way possible..."*

*Author: "Okay, just don't get carried away..."*

**It wasn't long before the newspaper reported the big news.**

*Local Billionaire Passes Away, Leaving Legacy of Philanthropy*

"Mr. Theodore, a prominent local millionaire known for his extensive philanthropic work, tragically passed away yesterday due to a sudden heart attack. The 78-year-old philanthropist breathed his last at one of the many homeless shelters he owned, a testament to his unwavering commitment to helping those in need.

Mr. Theodore's dedication to improving the lives of the less fortunate was unparalleled. However, his commitment to helping others did not end with his passing. In a surprising gesture, Mr. Theodore bequeathed his entire fortune, including his vast assets, to his teenage grandson, Murphy.

Theodore's passing has not only left a void in the world of philanthropy but also in the hearts of those who knew him. Colleagues, friends, and beneficiaries have come forward to share their fond memories of a man whose compassion, wisdom, and dedication touched so many lives.

As the community mourns the loss of this remarkable individual, it also celebrates the indelible impact he has made. Mr. Theodore's legacy will continue to inspire generations to come, reminding us all of the profound difference one person can make when driven by a genuine desire.

In honor of Mr. Theodore's memory, local leaders and organizations are planning a tribute event Wednesday morning to recognize and commemorate his extraordinary contributions."

*It was a cold rainy morning as many people in the community gathered to pay their respects to Mr. Theodore. The Author of course ditched school to attend this. However, he was confused. He looked all over and didn't see Murphy anywhere in sight. He thought to himself "Why isn't Murphy here?" Ms. Garcia also attended the ceremony. She walked up to The Author.*

*Author: "Hey Ms. G, Murphy, he isn't here."*

*Ms. Garcia: "There's something you should see..."*

*She pulled out her phone and showed him a clip of a news report that aired earlier in the morning. She pressed play on the video and a female reporter's voice began speaking...*

*"Good morning, while Murphy Theodore has not made a public statement on his grandfather's passing, he was seen last night and this morning occupying his grandfather's skyscraper known as Theodore Tower, which is located downtown in the city. According to eyewitness testimony, dozens of people has gone in and out of the multimillion dollar building in only the past few hours. We'll keep you updated as this story develops."*

*Ms. Garcia: "I woke up and saw this on the news."*

*Author: "What the hell is going on at that tower?"*

*Ms. Garcia: "I have no idea, but I can't believe he didn't come..."*

*Author: "Yeah, I think I better check up on him."*

*He took out his phone and typed a message to send in a group chat with The Short Kid and Damaris. He then sent the message.*

*"Guys, tonight we're heading on over to the city and going to Theodore Tower to see what's up with Murphy. Fill up your gas tank, Damaris."*

\*\*\*\*\*\*\*\*\*\*\*\*\*\*\*\*\*\*\*\*\*\*\*\*\*\*\*\*\*\*\*\*\*\*\*\*\*\*\*\*\*\*\*\*\*\*\*\*\*\*\*\*\*\*\*\*\*\*\*\*\*\*\*\*\*\*\*\*\*\*

*Randy was in his cell, anxiously preparing himself for what he was about to do. A cop came by and told him something.*

*"Alright, we're transferring you to the state prison in about 10 minutes!"*

*Randy: "I just have one question, where is all my stuff at?"*

*The cop responded, "In the evidence room, we aren't done inspecting all that."*

*Randy: "Oh okay, but hey really quickly can you come here for a second?"*

*"What is it punk?"*

*Randy: "I think I have something in my ear, could you possibly take a look?"*

*The cop walked up to the cell and Randy turned his head so the cop could look at his ear. He took out his flashlight and shined it in his ear.*

*"I don't see anything wrong."*

*Randy: "Keep looking."*

*Then, Randy put his arm through the metal bars, and slowly put his hand behind the cop's head. Then he rammed his head on the cell's metal bars repeatedly until the officer fell unconscious! Randy grabbed the cell keys off of the cop's utility belt and was able to unlock the door from inside! When the cell door opened, he knew it was showtime! He snatched the cop's gun and exited the holding area. Two cops were standing right outside the door!*

*"HEY!" the cops shouted! Randy hit them both on the head with the gun.*

*Randy: "Look sorry, but you all really fucked over the world."*

*Randy started to sneak around, and he tried his best not to be seen.*

*Randy: "I remember back in my time, we looted this abandoned police station. If I remember correctly the evidence room… shit. It was on the second floor."*

*Then suddenly a loud message played over the intercom throughout the entire building!*

*"AN INMATE HAS ESCAPED! LOCK ALL DOORS! SUSPECT IS ARMED AND DANGEROUS!"*

*Randy: "Damn it, they really about to do all this right now?"*

*A cop came from behind him and before the cop even said a word, he sucker punched him to sleep!*

*Randy: "Asshole."*

*He began running as fast as he could up the staircase! A few cops from nearby rooms came out and started to chase him!*

*Randy: "Is that all you pigs got?"*

*They then started firing their guns at him!*

*Randy: "Oh fuck!"*

*Randy ran as fast as he could! All the cops kept shooting but they missed every shot!*

*Randy: "With these types of shots, no wonder most of these guys were captured by Murphy's troops!"*

*He got up to the second-floor hallway, and he saw a glass vase with a flower in it. He picked it up and threw it down at some of the cops! It hit one of them, and the glass shattered everywhere! He had saved himself a bit of time and ran until he saw a door that said, 'Evidence Room.'*

*Randy: "Here it is!"*

*He opened the door and right on the table in the middle of the room, was all his stuff.*

*Randy: "BINGO!"*

*He grabbed his jetpack and put it on his back. He grabbed his blaster, and he even stole quite a few extra things like a police shield, brass knuckles, pepper spray, and knives. The cops were right outside the door, and then right away they knocked down the door! They opened fire on Randy, and he used the shield to protect himself from their bullets. He turned his jetpack on to the highest level and held the shield tight!*

*Randy: "You guys will thank me later!"*

*His jetpack went off and sent him flying through the room smashing directly into the cops! He was zooming fast, and the shield knocked out anyone who was in his way!*

*Randy: "THIS IS CRAZY!!!!"*

*He flew out the room and held the shield tight! He then smashed right through a glass window on the ceiling of the building that led to the roof outside! He kept flying upwards and he threw the shield down!*

*Randy: "YES, I ESCAPED, LET'S GO!"*

*He thought he was in the clear, until a police helicopter came out of nowhere and began chasing him through the sky!*

*Randy: "You have to be kidding me."*

*The helicopter had a machine gun on it, and it started firing at Randy like crazy! Randy was zooming through the sky at 80 MPH, nearly dodging each bullet! Despite his speed the helicopter was on his ass!*

*Randy: "Damn it, I've had enough of this!"*

*Randy flew straight up and flew above the helicopter to shoot the engine with his blaster! Tons of smoke started to come out of the helicopter, and it started to burn and crash down! The pilot inside was screaming for his life! Randy flew down quickly, broke the door on the helicopter, and pulled him out before the helicopter crashed!*

*Randy: "Even though you just tried to murder me I'm still going to save you!"*

*Randy safely threw the pilot down in a patch of grass, and he flew off, successfully escaping from the police station!*

*Randy: "Alright Randy, you've already wasted about 50 hours! It's time I finally find The Author, before it's too late!"*

*He flew high up into the sky!*

\*\*\*\*\*\*\*\*\*\*\*\*\*\*\*\*\*\*\*\*\*\*\*\*\*\*\*\*\*\*\*\*\*\*\*\*\*\*\*\*\*\*\*\*\*\*\*\*\*\*\*\*\*\*\*\*\*\*\*\*\*\*\*\*\*\*\*\*\*\*\*\*\*\*\*\*\*\*\*

*The Author was walking into an amusement park called 'Coffee Land!'*

*Author: "Yay! I'm so excited to be here!"*

*He walked into the park and the first thing he did was swim in the latte lake....*

*"Author wake the fuck up!"*

*The Author woke up in a panic! He was so confused and sweaty. It took him a moment to realize he was in the backseat of Damaris's car. Damaris was driving and The Short Kid was in the passenger seat.*

*Damaris: "Author you good man?"*

*Author: "Yeah, I just haven't slept good these past few nights, where are we going?"*

*Short Kid: "Remember, Theodore Tower?"*

*Author: "Oh yeah... I completely forgot for a second."*

*Damaris: "The GPS says we'll be there in a few minutes."*

*The Author looked out the window and saw that they had arrived in the city! The buildings in the nighttime sky were beautiful to look at.*

*Short Kid: "I can't believe Murphy is loaded now!"*

*Damaris: "For real man, like what's he going to do with all that money?"*

*The Author wasn't paying much attention to their conversation, there was too many things running through his mind...*

*Short Kid: "What do you think Author?"*

*Author: "I don't know, but guys, the other day at that event, that man who came in screaming, he said something about Murphy..."*

*Damaris: "So?"*

*Author: "I just thought it was weird, and now all this is happening."*

*Short Kid: "Yeah but to be honest it's probably nothing bro."*

*Author: "Yeah, I don't know. But Damaris..."*

*Damaris: "What's up?"*

*Author: "Why do you have all these bricks here in the backseat?"*

*Damaris: "Oh, me and my dad are going to resell them."*

*Author: "You are going to resell bricks? That doesn't make sense."*

*The GPS interrupted their conversation.*

*"Make a left turn and you'll arrive at your destination."*

*Author: "Okay boys we made it!"*

*Damaris turned left and they saw the building! It was huge!*

*Short Kid: "WOW!"*

*The skyscraper went up 98 floors high up in the sky! It was foggy outside, and they could not even see the top of the building!*

*Author: "I just can't believe he owns this!"*

*Short Kid: "This is insane!"*

*Damaris parked the car in front of the building and turned it off. The boys all hopped out of the car.*

*Damaris: "Did you tell him we were coming?"*

*Author: "Nah, but it's fine, he's my best friend."*

*They walked into the skyscraper that had the name Theodore written across the building in bright gold letters. The first floor was entirely pitch-black inside.*

*Short Kid: "Looks like this motherfucker didn't pay the electricity bill."*

*Damaris took out a flashlight and shined it all over the first floor.*

*Damaris: "Author, do you think he's even here?"*

*Author: "I feel like he is…"*

*They found a staircase and they decided to walk up! They were dying of exhaustion once they had walked up to the 30th floor!*

*Damaris: "Author! I don't think he's here!"*

*Short Kid was sweating so much and was still a floor below them.*

*Short Kid: "Guys, fuck this!"*

*He saw the door for the 29th floor, and he decided to open it. To his surprise, when he opened the door, he saw that the entire floor had electricity, and all the lights were on!*

*Short Kid: "Guys come down! I think I found something."*

*The Author and Damaris walked down, and they walked in the door with The Short Kid.*

*Author: "Why are all the lights on in here?"*

*The floor seemed completely empty, there was nothing or nobody in sight. They walked in a bit more until The Author noticed a door begin to open.*

*Author: "Uh oh."*

*A man walked out of the door, and it turns out it was just Murphy. He noticed the boys right away.*

*Murphy: "Oh hey guys, what a surprise!"*

*He was wearing an overpriced suit.*

*Author: "Yo Murphy!"*

*He walked up to them.*

*Murphy: "Wasn't expecting to see you today, Author."*

*Author: "Yeah man we just came to check up on you."*

*Murphy: "That's nice of you, but say did you guys walk up the stairs?"*

*Damaris: "Yeah, and all your power is out on most floors."*

*Murphy: "Yeah we turned some of the lights off."*

*Damaris: "Oh."*

*He pointed behind them and showed them the elevator.*

*Author: "Well, good to know that's there for when we leave."*

*Murphy: "Listen, Author can I talk to you privately in my office over here?"*

*Author: "Yeah sure. Guys, just stay out here and wait."*

*Short Kid: "Bruh."*

*The Author and Murphy walked into the room he had just walked out of. It was a huge office room. For some reason, probably over 50 men and women wearing all black clothing holding weapons were standing in there.*

*Author: "Uh, Murphy, who are all these people, are they your associates? Why are some of them holding rifles?"*

*Murphy: "Author, take a seat."*

*He sat down in a chair, and Murphy sat down at his desk with his arms folded together.*

*Murphy: "So what made you come all the way out here?"*

*Author: "Well bro, I know these past few hours have been crazy for you."*

*Murphy chuckled.*

*Murphy: "I wouldn't use the word crazy, more like, thrilling."*

*Author: "Yeah well um, you weren't at the ceremony this morning for your grandpa, and I was just wondering if you are all good?"*

*Murphy looked around at the other people in the room.*

*Murphy: "Would you all say I'm all good?"*

*A few of them all simultaneously said out loud...*

*"Yes!"*

*Murphy: "I'm doing just fine."*

*Author: "Oh, that's good."*

*The Author began to feel a bit uneasy.*

*Author: "I just wanted to see how you're feeling about your grandpa?"*

*Murphy stood up.*

*Murphy: "Author..."*

*He took a sip of water before he continued speaking.*

*Murphy: "You know for my whole life, I have always wanted to be just like him."*

*Author: "Yeah?"*

*Murphy: "Truthfully, I've always wanted to be better than him, and now I have that chance!"*

*Author: "Yeah you do, and you can keep his legacy strong!"*

*Murphy: "Mhm. I am preparing for a very important meeting this Friday at 2 AM."*

*The Author: "That's a really weird time to have a meeting. What's it about?"*

*Murphy: "Well, you are going to love this."*

*He took another slow sip of water before speaking.*

*Murphy: "As you know my grandfather owned a few shelters around the state, and even a few orphanages here in the city."*

*Author: "Yes, he did such great things in those buildings."*

*The Author felt the tension in the room.*

*Murphy: "Mhm."*

*Murphy took another slow sip of water...*

*Murphy: "How rude of me for not asking, would you like a glass of water?"*

*Author: "Sure."*

*One of his men poured him a glass of water and handed it to him.*

*Murphy: "As a businessman yourself Author, you know sometimes you have to make sacrifices, right?"*

*Author: "I guess."*

*Murphy: "Well, those little buildings my grandfather operated, don't fit my current plans..."*

*Author: "What do you mean?"*

*Murphy chuckled.*

*Murphy: "All of those shitty little buildings, I will be selling them on Friday..."*

*Author: "Wait... what?"*

*The Author started getting nervous.*

*Murphy: "I will be selling all those buildings and they will be demolished."*

*Author knew he had to speak up.*

*Author: "But Murphy, you can't do that!?"*

*Murphy: "Why not?"*

*Author: "Because, you can't just throw out all those people who live in the shelters and orphanages!"*

*Murphy's demeanor started to change.*

*Author: "Dude, don't you understand, if you do that, and throw out all those people who live in those buildings, they'll be laying in the street without food or water. Murphy... those people, without the assistance, they'll die."*

*Murphy smiled and took a sip of water.*

*Murphy: "Then so be it."*

*The Author was in a state of shock, "This can't be real!" he thought to himself.*

*Murphy: "This is all build up for my true plan."*

*He stood up from his desk and looked out the window. He was staring down at the people walking the streets of the city.*

*Murphy: "I'm building an army, Author."*

*He turned around to face him.*

*Murphy: "I'm using my newfound fortune to pay the meanest crooks out there to join my crew, and trust me people will do anything for money..."*

*The Author was beginning to panic!*

*Murphy: "This is a plan that will take decades to execute..."*

*Murphy: "First my troops will take over the streets of this city, then, we'll take over the entire state, and finally we will take over the entire country! THEN, MY ARMY WILL BE BIG ENOUGH TO RULE THE ENTIRE WORLD!"*

*He threw down his water and glass shattered everywhere! The Author couldn't comprehend what he was hearing!*

*Murphy: "We're going to invade and conquer it all, and anybody who tries to stop me, will get run over in the process! I WILL BE BETTER THAN MY GRANDPA EVER WAS!"*

*The Author: "Murphy, I can't believe this! You have to be joking?"*

*Murphy: "Author, join me."*

*Author: "What?"*

*Murphy: "Yes, join me, and together we will take over the world!"*

*Author: "Murphy, you are fucking crazy!"*

*Murphy: "What do you mean, I thought we was cool?"*

*Author: "YOU ARE A FUCKING CRAZY MANIAC!"*

*The Author stood up!*

*Author: "YOU HAVE LOST YOUR MIND!"*

*Murphy was getting VERY MAD!*

*Author: "First, closing the buildings is fucked up, and then you want to create an army and to conquer the world?"*

*Those people in the room, now to The Author's knowledge of them actually being Murphy's troops began to put their hands on their holsters and weapons.*

*Author: "I don't know what you think your about to do but it's not going to happen, someone will stop you, this will never happen!"*

*Murphy walked towards him.*

*Murphy: "Listen here…"*

*He approached The Author and punched him right in the gut!*

*Murphy: "Nobody will be able to stop me, so either fall in line, or you'll die with the rest of them."*

*He hit The Author pretty hard!*

*Author: "You won't get away with this!"*

*He took his glass of water and slammed it over Murphy's head, causing him to bleed! He looked over at all the troops getting ready to attack him, but before they could do anything he ran out the hallway to Short Kid and Damaris.*

*"Should we get him?"*

*Murphy: "Yes... kill him!"*

*The boys saw The Author sprinting out of the room!*

*Damaris: "Author, what's wrong?"*

*Author: "RUN FOR YOUR LIVES!"*

*Damaris and Short Kid turned around and saw the huge group of troops about to chase after them!*

*Short Kid: "WHAT THE FUCK!"*

*They all took off and ran as fast as they could! The Author opened the elevator and held it open for his friends!*

*Author: "HURRY!"*

*They all jumped in the elevator and the troops were running towards them! Luckily with a second to spare, the elevator door closed before any of them could get the boys!*

*Damaris: "AUTHOR WHAT IS GOING ON?"*

*Author was panicking.*

*Author: "MURPHY HAS GONE CRAZY OR SOMETHING, I DON'T KNOW!"*

*The elevator got to the first floor and the doors opened and they began to book it again!*

*Author: "JUMP IN THE CAR AS FAST AS POSSIBLE!"*

*The troops ran down the stairs and were on their tail! One of the troops cocked a gun and fired at the boys, almost hitting The Short Kid!*

*Short Kid: "OH MY WHAT THE HELL!!!!"*

*They ran out the main door and jumped in the car.*

*Author: "DAMARIS, DRIVE!"*

*Damaris started the car and pulled off! The troops ran out the building and fired a few shots at the car that hit the back windshield!*

*Damaris: "Oh fuck, oh fuck, oh fuck!"*

*The troops started dispersing and were hopping into cars and motorcycles that were branded with the name Murphy on them.*

*Short Kid: "WE ARE GOING TO FUCKING DIE!"*

*The troops started racing towards their car!*

*Author: "THEY ARE TRYING TO KILL US!"*

*A truck full of troops sped up to the right side of their car and started to ram into them, they almost ran them off the road!*

*Short Kid: "STEP ON IT DAMARIS!"*

*Damaris stomped his foot on the gas!*

*The Author was in the backseat when he saw the troops on bikes pull up!*

*Author: "SHIT!"*

*They began to pull up attempting to surround them.*

*Short Kid: "WHAT DO WE DO?"*

*The Author remembered the bricks in the back seat, so he picked them all up and handed a few to Short Kid!*

*Author: "Throw these at them!"*

*They opened their windows and began chucking the bricks at the troops. Author threw a few and knocked the people off the bikes! Short Kid tossed a brick at the car trying to run them off the road, and it ended up crashing through their front windshield and it hit the driver of the car! The troop lost control of the car and crashed! Damaris was trying his best to maintain control of the car while the other troops were still after them!*

*Author: "THERE'S MORE OF THEM COMING, AND WE'RE ALL OUT OF BRICKS!"*

*Another truck filled with troops pulled up to the left side of the car, and one of the troops screamed out at them!*

*"THIS ONE IS A PERSONAL GESTURE FROM THE BOSS!"*

*Damaris: "What is that supposed to mean?!"*

*They threw something at the car and it broke through the back seat window. The Author knew exactly what it was once he saw it land next to him!*

*Author: "GUYS, JUMP OUT THE CAR IT'S A GRENADE!"*

*Damaris and Short Kid: "WHAT!?"*

*Author: "JUMP NOW!!!!!!!!!!!"*

*They all opened their doors while the car was going 100 MPH and jumped out onto the hard pavement road! The car crashed into a building AND EXPLODED! They each had terrible cuts and bumps on them. They were bleeding a bit.*

*Author: "Are you guys okay?"*

*Damaris: "Barely."*

*Short Kid: "AH FUCK THAT HURT!"*

*They were all lying in the street in extreme pain when the troops pulled up and hopped out of their vehicles. One of the female troops approached them and kicked The Short Kid!*

*"Pathetic, I almost feel bad that we have to kill you boys..."*

*Damaris: "NO PLEASE!"*

*Short Kid: "PLEASE DON'T, MY FAMILY, NO!"*

*She responded to them after chuckling.*

*"Say your prayers boys."*

*Then all the troops took out their guns and pointed it at them! All the boys could think about was their loved ones...*

*Author: "Goodbye you guys..."*

*They all started to cry as they knew the end was near. The lady said...*

*"On the count of three, open fire!"*

*"1"*

*Damaris: "Goodbye...."*

*"2"*

*Short Kid: "I love you guys..."*

*They all closed their eyes, and braced themselves for the count of 3, until...*

*"Who is that?"*

*"What the hell?"*

*The Author opened his eyes, and they began to fire their weapons at a mysterious figure hidden in the shadows...*

*Author: "Who are they shooting at?"*

*The mysterious figure walked towards the troops. They kept firing at the person, but it appeared that each shot did not affect them at all. The troops became frightened when they saw their bullets weren't working...*

*Short Kid: "Dude, Damaris, you know who I bet that is?"*

*Damaris: "There's no way..."*

*The mysterious figure came out of the shadows. It was a man who was wearing a hoodie with a dark grey jumpsuit under it, with black gloves on his hands, black boots on his feet, and a gas mask covering his face.*

*Short Kid: "HOLY SHIT IT'S THE PYROMANIAC!"*

*The troops continued to shoot at him, and the one trooper lady said something in a frighten tone!*

*"KEEP SHOOTING UNTIL YOU KILL HIM!"*

*The PyroManiac balled up his fists and flew towards the troop lady and knocked her face in! The other troops ran out of ammo, and Pyro ran up to one of them and punched him over 5 times! The man's blood was all over his hands.*

*Short Kid: "THIS IS SO COOL!*

*Some of the other troops began to retreat, but PyroManiac wasn't done yet. He flew towards another one of the troops and grabbed him by the shirt. He flew upwards high in the sky and the troop began to panic!*

*PyroManiac: "WHO DO YOU WORK FOR?"*

*Fear began to consume the man.*

*"MURPHY, MURPHY!"*

*Author: "What the hell is going on up there?"*

*PyroManiac: "DON'T FUCKIN LIE TO ME, WHO DO YOU WORK FOR?!"*

*The troop acted like a scared baby.*

*"I'm telling you the truth! His name is Murphy Theodore!"*

*PyroManiac: "Hm..."*

*He dropped the troop from high up in the sky, and the troop screamed until the moment he hit the ground!*

*Damaris: "WOAH DUDE!"*

*PyroManiac flew back down to the ground, and he thought the fight was over, until a gang of troops showed up with chains, baseball bats, and knives.*

*"HE'S RESISTANT TO ANYTHING RELATED TO FIRE, THESE WEAPONS SHOULD DO THE TRICK!"*

*They all began to charge at him! PyroManiac groaned in annoyance. A troop ran up to him and swung the bat at him! He dodged it and knocked the troop out with a sweet uppercut! Two of them attempted to gang up on him with chains, and they began swinging them at him. One of them hit him in the leg, and Pyro looked over at the troop... At that moment, the troop knew he fucked up. He flew towards the troop and slammed him into the pavement! The other troop with a chain dropped it and put his hands up! Pyro spared him...*

*Author: "PYROMANIAC LOOK OUT!"*

*The troop with a knife stabbed PyroManiac in the back! PyroManiac's orange aura glowed very brightly as he slowly turned around to the troop that stabbed him. Pyro was breathing heavy like a mad dog. He then tossed the troop into a nearby building! Pyro pulled the knife out his back. He held it in his hand and threw it directly at the head of another troop who was charging towards the boys! The troop fell to the ground with blood gushing from his head.*

*PyroManiac: "I think that's all of them."*

*Then, a van with 10 more troops pulled up.*

*"KILL THE PYROMANIAC!"*

*PyroManiac: "Fuckin' Christ!"*

*They all jumped out of the van and were ready to gang up on him! They all began to charge at him, when suddenly he flew up in the air and flew out of their sight!*

*"Where did he go?"*

*The boys were watching all of this in complete shock, and they saw he flew behind their van they just pulled up in. Pyro then picked up the van using all his strength and threw it at the crowd of troopers, crushing most of them.*

*Short Kid: "DAMN THAT'S FUCKED UP!"*

*Author: "Yeah, I sure didn't expect to see this today."*

*The PyroManiac was getting a bit tired, when he saw 4 more troopers were still ready to fight!*

*The Author slowly walked over.*

*Author: "Listen goons, I'd suggest you just leave."*

*PyroManiac: "Don't ruin the fun..."*

*Author: "Sorry man, do your thing."*

*The troops ran towards The PyroManiac with full force! Pyro grabbed one of the guys and threw him so far up in the sky nobody could even see him!*

*Short Kid: "Damn where did that dude go?"*

*The other 3 guys jumped on him all at once! Pyro pulled one of the guys off of him, threw him to the ground and stomped on his leg!*

*"AHHHH!"*

*The other two guys backed off a bit but weren't done. One of the troops put on a steel gauntlet and started punching PyroManiac as hard as he could! Pyro then grabbed his hand midway through the man's punch and snapped his wrist while his hand was in the gauntlet!*

*"FUCK!"*

*The troop backed down and ran away. There was only one trooper remaining. He was ready to keep going, until a rock hit his head and he fell to the ground!*

*Short Kid: "I GOT HIM!"*

*The PyroManiac was super tired after that long brawl. Then all of a sudden, he heard cop sirens going off like crazy. He turned around to face the boys.*

*PyroManiac: "We need to get out of here, follow me!"*

*The PyroManiac started running through a nearby alleyway and the boys followed him.*

*Short Kid "I can't believe I'm hanging out with The PyroManiac right now!"*

*They ran to an abandoned building and Pyro broke down the door. They all ran inside the building to avoid the police from finding them.*

*PyroManiac: "Why were those people attacking you?"*

*Damaris: "Yeah Author, what the hell happened when you went into Murphy's office?!"*

*Short Kid: "For real, why did those people just try to kill us?!"*

*Author: "Alright, I'll explain it all."*

*******************************************************************

*Natasha rang the doorbell at Riley's house. Riley opened the door and gave Natasha a hug.*

*Riley: "Thanks for coming over so late Nat, please come in."*

*She walked in and they both sat down on the couch.*

*Natasha: "No problem, is everything okay?"*

*Riley: "I don't know, Author told me he was going to the city tonight, and I haven't heard anything from him or any of his friends in hours!"*

*Natasha: "That's so not like him at all."*

*Riley: "I know, and have you seen the news?"*

*Natasha: "No what happened?"*

*Riley: "Apparently near Theodore Tower there was a huge high-speed chase involving like 8 cars, and they said there was like 40 casualties!"*

*Natasha: "Oh my goodness!"*

*Riley: "And I just have a feeling..."*

*Natasha: "What feeling?"*

*Riley: "I feel like something is wrong, I'm worried about him. I just, feel like he was there or something, or worse, is a victim."*

*She began to cry.*

*Natasha: "Listen, I know that he's smart enough to get himself out of any situation."*

*Riley: "I know, but it's not like him to not answer any of my calls or texts."*

*Natasha: "Listen, I'll stay here with you until you hear back from him, okay?"*

*Riley: "Thank you Nat, do you want to just spend the night?"*

*Natasha: "Sure, I'm cool with that, let's watch a movie or something.
Riley: "Sounds good!"*

*Natasha: "Ease your mind, he's probably just fine."*

\*\*\*\*\*\*\*\*\*\*\*\*\*\*\*\*\*\*\*\*\*\*\*\*\*\*\*\*\*\*\*\*\*\*\*\*\*\*\*\*\*\*\*\*\*\*\*\*\*\*\*\*\*\*\*\*\*\*\*\*\*\*\*\*\*\*\*\*\*\*

*Ms. Garcia was driving in her car late at night after running some errands. She was down the block from the shelter, so she decided to drive over there out of boredom. She pulled up outside and got out of her car to stretch her legs and look at the building.*

*Ms. Garcia: "I can't believe that Mr. Theodore is actually gone…"*

*She was staring at the building deep in her thoughts, when she noticed something odd. There were two people standing on the roof of the shelter holding guns!*

*Ms. Garcia: "What the hell?"*

*She walked up a bit closer, when she heard people walking by!*

*Ms. Garcia: "Oh shit."*

*She jumped in a random bush and hid. Two people in all black were walking by chatting.*

114

*"You ready for this Friday?"*

*"You know it!"*

*Ms. Garcia was confused but kept listening in.*

*"Yeah, once the boss is done selling all these shitty shelters and whatever, he's going to collect the money and hire more of us."*

*Ms. Garcia thought to herself "WAIT, MURPHY IS GOING TO SELL THE SHELTERS?!"*

*"Yep, and once he does that, that's when the invasion will begin."*

*"I'm so ready for this!"*

*Ms. Garcia: "Invasion?"*

*"It's a flawless plan, there will be way too many of us and we will outnumber anyone who tries to stop us!"*

*"Yeah, the police or military won't have nothing on us!"*

*"The world will be under our control!"*

*Ms. Garcia began to panic! She couldn't comprehend what was happening. Her breathing got louder and louder.*
*"You hear something?"*

*"Yeah, it sounded like it came from those bushes over."*

*Ms. Garcia thought to herself "Oh fuck, run!" So, she jumped out of the bushes and began to run!*

*"HEY STOP THAT LADY!"*

*She tried to run back to her car as fast as possible, and the two troops chased after her! She tried to open her car door, but before she could, one of the troops tackled her to the ground!*

*Ms. Garcia: "HELP! HELP!"*

*The troop hit her in the head with their gun, and she passed out!*

*"What should we do with her?"*

*"Let's take her to headquarters."*

*"I'm sorry, where is that again?"*

*"Theodore Tower."*

*"Oh yeah."*

*The troops threw her in the back of a van and took her to Theodore Tower where she would be held captive!*

*****************************************************************
*Author: "And pretty much that's everything that went down."*

*Short Kid: "Wait, so let me get this straight, Murphy is paying all those people because he is going to try to overpower everyone and control the world?"*

*Author: "Yeah..."*

*Damaris: "I just can't believe this is real."*

*PyroManiac: "This Murphy guy reminds me of this one scum I've dealt with sometime ago... and you said that he owns a bunch of buildings?"*

*Author: "Yeah, his grandfather Mr. Theodore use to operate these homeless shelters, and quite a few orphanages around here..."*

*PyroManiac: "You fuckin' serious?"*

*Author: "Yeah."*

*PyroManiac's breathing started to get a bit tense.*

*Author: "What is it?"*

*PyroManiac: "I met his grandfather before..."*

*Author: "You did!?"*

*PyroManiac: "Yes, he owned the orphanage that I grew up in!"*

*The boys were shocked.*
*PyroManiac: "And this fucker is going to shut it down?!"*

*Pyro got heated and he decided to punch the cement wall a few times out of anger! He made a few pretty good dents in the wall.*

*PyroManiac: "When is the meeting!?"*

*Author: "Friday at 2 AM."*

*PyroManiac: "Okay, I'll be there, and I'll deal with him."*

*Author: "No the fuck you aren't."*

*Pyro turns to The Author in a 'What did you just say to me?' kind of way. The rest of the crew, even The Author, got a bit shook on how Pyromaniac reacted.*

*Short Kid: "Author, are you serious right now?"*

*Damaris: "Yeah, he legit just tried to kill you! I don't get why you are being so forgiving."*

*Author: "Because, I've grown up with that dude since we were babies, he was my best friend, and if you try to kill him, then truly you are just as bad as him."*

*Short Kid: "Bro Pyro can you tell him to shut the hell up!?"*

*The PyroManiac was thinking for a minute.*

*PyroManiac: "So you say he was your best friend?"*

*Author: "Yes, and despite everything, I don't want to lose him..."*

*PyroManiac: "I get it."*

*Damaris and Short Kid were shocked when he said that!*

*PyroManiac: "I lost my best friend. He died right in front of me... I would not wish that pain I felt on anyone else."*

*Damaris: "I get that, but he might take over the world and try to kill us all!"*

*PyroManiac thought for a second.*

*PyroManiac: "Tell me, do you have a plan, Author?"*

*Author: "No, I don't... but I can make one up!"*

*He thought of something quickly.*

*Author: "Listen, Friday, help me and the guys break into the building and get me through the troops, and I'll talk to Murphy before he officially sells the buildings. I can change his mind before he does anything crazy!"*

*Damaris: "That is the lamest idea I have ever heard!"*

*Short Kid: "I'm in."*
*Damaris: "Are you serious?"*

*Author: "And Pyro, if my plan doesn't work, do what you need to do…"*

*The PyroManiac thought about it for a second. He usually doesn't play by other people's rules, but he felt sympathetic. He wanted to save the orphanage, but he didn't want to kill Author's friend.*

*PyroManiac: "I'm in."*

*Damaris: "You too?!"*

*PyroManiac: "Yes, but if things don't work out the way you want, I'll deal with it myself."*

*Author: "Deal."*

*Damaris: "This is crazy."*

*Author: "Damaris, you in bro?"*

*Damaris took a pause.*

*Damaris: "I, um… okay, yeah, I'm in!"*

*Short Kid: "Yessir, me, the boys, and Pyro about to save the world!"*

*PyroManiac: "Author, here's my phone number."*

*He handed The Author a piece of paper with his number on it.*

*PyroManiac: "I'll see you all Friday!"*

*The PyroManiac looked up and flew right through the roof of the abandoned building they were in!*

*Short Kid: "OMG THAT WAS SO COOL DID YOU GUYS SEE HOW HE JUST FLEW THROUGH LIKE THAT!"*

*Author: "It's time to be serious Short Kid."*

*Short Kid: "Okay sorry, it was just cool."*

*Damaris: "Hey guys, how are we going to get home?"*

*Short Kid: "Oh yeah, your car exploded..."*

*Author: "I'm sorry about that Damaris."*

*Damaris: "I'll deal with it later."*

*Author: "I will call my guy to come pick us up."*

*When he took out his phone to call The Cruiser, he saw he had 37 missed calls from Riley. But worse, he had 50 missed calls from his mom.*

*Author: "Oh shit."*

THURSDAY

*It was 1 AM, and Natasha was sitting in Riley's room watching a romance movie called True Lover that was based on a true story. She was stuffing popcorn in her face, when she heard Riley coming back from the bathroom.*

*Riley: "Hey Nat, Author just called me..."*

*Natasha: "What did he say?"*

*Riley: "You are not going to believe me what he just told me..."*

*Natasha: "Why not?"*

*Riley: "It's about Murphy."*

*Natasha was visibly confused, and Riley told her everything....*

\*\*\*\*\*\*\*\*\*\*\*\*\*\*\*\*\*\*\*\*\*\*\*\*\*\*\*\*\*\*\*\*\*\*\*\*\*\*\*\*\*\*\*\*\*\*\*\*\*\*\*\*\*\*\*\*\*\*\*\*\*\*\*\*

*Author: "Alright guys, I called Riley and told her everything."*

*Damaris: "That's good bro."*

*Author: "Hey Cruiser, thanks for picking us up so late."*

*The Cruiser: "Nah man don't even worry about it. I was chilling with this 500-pound girl, and I needed an excuse to leave."*

*Author: "Oh alright."*

*The boys were all in the SUV and they all closed their eyes and fell asleep for a bit while The Cruiser drove them out of the city. He took home Short Kid first, then Damaris. The last stop was Author's house.*

*The Cruiser: "Hey, wake up!"*

*He woke up in a panic!*

*Author: "Oh, thank you man!"*

*The Cruiser: "No problem, get some rest bro you had a crazy night."*

*Author: "Thanks, goodnight!"*

*He closed the door of the SUV, and The Cruiser drove off. He walked up to his front door and dug in his pockets for his keys. Suddenly, he heard footsteps coming from behind him. He turned around and it was Randy standing there.*

*Author: "Hey it's you!"*

*Randy came at him slowly with his hands up.*

*Randy: "Author, we got off on the wrong foot, my name is Randy..."*

*Author: "What did you say!?"*

*The Author walked closer to him.*

*Author: "What did you say the other day? You said something about Murphy, right?!"*

*Randy: "That's what I want to talk to you about. There is something I'm going to tell you, and you might not believe me, but please listen to me."*

*Author: "I'm all ears man."*

*Randy: "Okay, this is going to sound crazy. But I am from the future…"*

*The Author stared at him in confusion.*

*Randy: "I come from a dystopian world 30 years in the future, where your friend Murphy…"*

*Author: "Let me guess, hires soldiers, creates an army, and takes over the world?"*

*Randy was shocked that The Author said that.*

*Randy: "Uh, yeah. How did you know?"*

*Author: "You have no idea what I been through tonight… his grandpa died now he's acting like a fucking idiot!"*

*Randy: "Oh no… he's already got the money?"*

*Author: "Uh, yeah, since yesterday."*

*Randy: "Oh no, we might be too late…"*

*Author: "Don't worry, I think I have a plan…"*

*Randy: "But wait, you believe me that I'm from the future?"*

*Author: "Well after everything I've been through today it wouldn't be the craziest thing I've heard. And you did kinda warn us about Murphy. But I need to know, what happens to me in the future?"*

*Randy: "I can't tell you… but please, we must hurry and stop him before he does any more damage."*

*Author: "Okay, let's talk about this more in the morning dude, I am exhausted."*

*The Author turned his back on Randy and began to unlock his front door.*

*Randy: "HEY! I hate to ask, but I have nowhere to go, can I crash at your place?"*

*The Author let out a sigh.*

*Author: "Sure."*

*Randy: "Great, we can stay up all night and plan!"*

*Author: "NO I NEED TO SLEEP FIRST!"*

*He opened the door and they both walked in. They took two steps in the door when the lights suddenly turned on. The Author's parents were sitting in the living room waiting for him!*

*Author's Mom: "Where have you been?"*

*Author's Dad: "We've been freaking out!"*

*Author: "I'm sorry, I had a long day…"*

*Author's Mom: "Are you okay, you look like your hurt?!"*

*Author: "Yea, I'm fine."*

*Author's Dad: "Who's your friend?"*

*Author: "Oh this is, you said your name is Randy right?"*

*Randy shook his head yes and his parents were confused.*

*Author: "He's just going to spend the night."*

*His mom got up from the couch.*

*Author's Mom: "What's been going on with you? You've been ditching school, and you haven't been enjoying your last week of high school it seems like."*

*Author: "I, have no idea how to explain it…"*

*Author's Mom: "Okay, son."*

*His dad then spoke up.*

*Author's Dad: "There's something we need to tell you…"*

*He could tell by his dad's tone something was wrong.*

*Author: "What happened?"*

*Author's Dad: "Your friend, Ms. Garcia, was seen being abducted a few hours ago near the shelter your friend owns."*

*The Author and Randy were shocked!*

*Author: "WHAT!?"*

*Randy: "LINDA GOT KIDNAPPED?"*

*Author's Mom: "It's true, she still lives at home with her parents, and they reported her missing not long ago."*

*Author: "What the hell…"*

*Author's Dad: "A witness who saw this happened came forward, now it's all over the news."*

*Randy: "Holy shit!"*

*******************************************************************

*It was 3 AM, and Ms. Garcia had just woken up after being knocked out. She was handcuffed to a railing in an empty room, and she had no clue where she was…*

*Ms. Garcia: "WHERE THE FUCK AM I?"*

*She tried breaking free, but to no avail. Murphy was standing outside the door talking to one of his troops.*

*Murphy: "WHAT THE HELL DO YOU MEAN THE AUTHOR AND HIS FRIENDS GOT AWAY?"*

*"They did, and sir, the media is reporting on the high-speed chase, they might catch on to us before Friday. We need to lay low…"*

*Murphy checked the troop!*

*Murphy: "Don't tell me what to do!"*

*"Sorry sir."*

*Murphy: "Whatever, once my true plans begin, they won't survive very long…"*

*"However, another group of troops caught a woman snooping around the one shelter and brought her here."*

*Murphy: "Let me see her."*

*He walked to the room Ms. Garcia was being held in, and the moment he opened the door he immediately recognized her.*

*Murphy: "Ms. Garcia, wow, shocking to see you here."*

*Ms. Garcia: "LET ME OUT OF HERE!"*

*Murphy: "I can't do that, you'll snitch."*

*Ms. Garcia: "You're a monster, your plan of attacking and becoming a ruler of territory, will never work!"*

*Murphy: "Shut up! My army will be unstoppable! Once I get those damn buildings off my hands, I'll have enough money to hire enough troops till the end of time!"*

*Ms. Garcia: "I swear, I am willing to spend the rest of my life fighting you!"*

*Murphy: "You will never beat me!"*

*Ms. Garcia was incredibly scared for what was to come.*

*Murphy: "Once I complete the deal Friday morning, the invasion will officially begin!"*

*Ms. Garcia: "You are NOTHING like your grandfather..."*

*Murphy: "DON'T COMPARE HIM TO ME, I AM BETTER THAN HIM!"*

*She then spit on him! And Murphy smacked her in the face! It left a huge handprint on her cheek!*

*Murphy: "Bitch."*

*He began walking out of the room in visible frustration, and as he was leaving Ms. Garcia started to scream at him!*

*Ms. Garcia: "THE AUTHOR WILL STOP YOU! HE WON'T LET YOU GET AWAY WITH THIS!"*

*Before he left the room, he said something under his breath...*

*Murphy: "He's welcome to try."*

*He turned off the lights in the room and shut the door on her.*

\*\*\*\*\*\*\*\*\*\*\*\*\*\*\*\*\*\*\*\*\*\*\*\*\*\*\*\*\*\*\*\*\*\*\*\*\*\*\*\*\*\*\*\*\*\*\*\*\*\*\*\*\*\*\*\*\*\*\*\*\*\*\*\*\*\*

*Riley and Natasha were still awake. Riley checked the time on her phone.*

*Riley: "It's 4 in the morning Nat."*

*Natasha: "I can't sleep..."*

*Riley: "Same, I just can't believe what's going on."*

*Natasha: "Why would Murphy want to take over the world?"*

*Riley: "I don't know, this all doesn't make any sense!"*

*Natasha: "That money changed him."*

*Riley walked over to the window in her bedroom that faced out to the street, and she began just thinking deeply about everything.*

*Riley: "If only..."*

*Natasha: "If only what?"*

*Riley didn't respond, and Natasha was confused, so she looked over at Riley. She noticed Riley was staring out at something...*

*Natasha: "What is it, Riley?"*

*Riley: "It looks like there's a man standing outside holding a gun?"*

*Natasha came to the window and saw the man too.*

*Natasha: "What the hell."*

*Riley: "I'm going to crack the window open a bit."*

*She slowly and quietly opened her window just a tiny bit, so they'd be able to hear the man outside. He began speaking to someone over a walkie talkie.*

*"I'm telling you when the plan begins, this whole street will belong to us! I'm definitely going to live in one of these houses!"*

*Riley and Natasha looked on in shock!*

*Riley: "No..."*

*Natasha: "This is happening way too fast!"*

*Riley: "Wait shhh."*

*"Yep, just a few more days, but hey, did you hear some of the other guys found this lady named Linda Garcia snooping around the shelter?"*

*They kept on listening closely.*

*"Yeah, they snatched her up and took her to Theodore Tower..."*

*Riley was stunned!*

*Riley: "OMG! They took Ms. Garcia?!!"*

*Natasha: "I'm starting to freak out..."*

*Riley: "That's it!"*

*She stood up and headed downstairs.*

*Natasha: "What are you doing?!"*

*She ran down the stairs and headed for the front door. She grabbed a coffee mug that was sitting in her living room and headed outside!*

*Natasha: "THIS IS CRAZY, STOP!"*

*Riley walked out the front door and slowly headed towards the man who was still talking to a friend.*

*"And yeah, the boss told me to just patrol this area for right now."*

*She slowly walked up to the man from behind. When she got right behind him, she raised the coffee mug above his head and smashed it right over him! He fell to the ground and became unconscious! She grabbed his walkie talkie and ran back into her house!*

*Natasha: "OH MY GOD THAT WAS INSANE!"*

*Riley: "Hey, those people tried to just murder my boyfriend, they deserved that!"*

*Natasha was flabbergasted!*

*Riley: "I grabbed his walkie talkie!"*

*"Sir, are you still there?"*

*Riley responded to the man.*

*Riley: "We're coming for you stupid fascists!"*

*She threw it on the ground and smashed it with her foot!*

*Natasha: "Wow."*

*****************************************************************

*The Author was sleeping on his couch, when he woke up to the smell of a fresh cup of coffee on the table next to him. He woke up and took a sip of it. He noticed Randy sitting next to him.*

*Randy: "Hey bud, I made you a fresh cup of coffee."*

*Author: "Oh, thanks!"*

*He let out a big yawn and took another sip of his coffee.*

*Author: "Man, what time is it?"*

*Randy: "It's 5:30 in the morning."*

*Author: "UGHHH!"*

*Randy: "Author, I know you are tired, but we need to act fast!"*

*Author: "Alright, I'm waking up."*

*He stretched his arms out and yawned. He was feeling a bit sore after jumping out of the car last night.*

*Randy: "Hey I took a shower after you fell asleep, is it cool that I used the red towel in the bathroom?"*

*Author: "I'm pretty sure that's my brother's towel."*

*Randy: "Oh."*

*The Author finished his coffee and stood up.*

*Author: "So, I'm just curious, but how did you travel back in time?"*

*Randy: "My commander had some crazy device that was able to send me back in time 30 years."*

*Author: "Oh wow, who was your commander?"*

*Randy didn't want to tell him it was Damaris, so he was very vague with his answer.*

*Randy: "He was a good man, who sacrificed his life for the entire world."*

*Author: "That's great. I'm still just trying to process everything that's going on..."*

*Randy: "I get it, I'm sure you aren't used to this type of stuff..."*

*Author: "Yeah. But wait, I just have to ask, why did you come looking for me specifically?"*

*Randy stood up.*

*Randy: "Author, I was told to come find you..."*

*Author: "That's pretty sus man."*

*Randy: "Listen Author, I was told that you were the only one who can stop him!"*

*Author: "Well thanks man, that totally didn't just put a ton of pressure on me."*

*Randy: "It's true, you even said last night that you had a plan."*

*Author: "Yeah, it involves me, my friend Damaris, my friend The Short Kid, this fire superhero guy, and I'm assuming you too?"*

*Randy: "Ok, that's a start."*

*Author: "We need to find more people, but first we need to figure out where Ms. G is!"*

*Suddenly, they heard a knock at the door! They both were startled, and Randy took out his blaster ready to defend himself! The Author slowly walked to the door and looked out of the peephole.*

*Author: "Calm down, it's just two of my friends!"*

*He put his blaster away in his pocket and The Author opened the door for Riley and Natasha!*

*Author: "What are you guys doing-?!"*

*Riley ran up to him and gave him a hug!*

*Riley: "Are you okay?!"*

*Author: "Yes, I'm perfectly fine."*

*Natasha: "Author, Ms. Garcia has been kidnapped!"*

*Randy chimed in!*

*Randy: "WE KNOW!"*

*Natasha was confused as fuck when she saw him.*

*Natasha: "Uh Author, why is that crazy guy from the event in your house?!"*

*Author: "I'll explain all of that later!"*

*Riley: "They took her to Theodore Tower!"*

*Author: "WHAT!"*

*Natasha: "Yes! We overheard one of Murphy's guys talking about it, he was near Riley's house!"*

*Riley: "Yeah, and I took his ass out!"*

*Author: "OMG ARE YOU OKAY?"*

*Riley: "I'm chilling don't worry."*

*Author: "Listen guys…"*

*He took a dramatic pause.*

*Author: "We're about to go to war if we don't do something…"*

*Randy: "Believe me, worse than you could ever imagine…"*

*The girls were confused.*

*Author: "In less than 24 hours, me and a few friends are going to put an end to this, and Riley…"*

*He looked her in the eyes.*

*Author: "I don't know what's going to happen. This can end really bad for me, but we need to stop him, and I'm sorry but I won't let you convince me not to."*

*Riley: "Author, I would never tell you to not do this..."*

*Natasha: "I'm in!"*

*Author: "Are you serious?"*

*Riley: "Me too!"*

*The Author smirked and turned back to Randy.*

*Author: "Let's assemble a team, then we'll be ready to go stop him..."*

■■■■■■■■■■■■■■■■■■■■■■■■■■■■■■■■■■■■■■■■■■■

*Class had begun and Mr. Bill sat down in his chair.*

*Mr. Bill: "Where the hell has The Author been?"*

*Marcus was sitting down at his desk unbelievably bored. He thought to himself "I can't wait to graduate in two days."*

*Mr. Bill: "HEY THERE YOU ARE!"*

*Marcus saw The Author standing in the doorway staring at him.*

*Author: "Marcus, we need you man…"*

*Mr. Bill and the class sat there confused.*

*Marcus: "Okay then."*

*He stood up and headed out the door in his sweaty white tank top.*

*Mr. Bill: "HEY ASSHAT WHERE ARE YOU GOING?!"*

*Marcus walked out the door and ignored the teacher.*

*Mr. Bill: "DAMN IT BOY YOU BETTER ANSWER ME!"*

*They both ran out the school and The Author caught him up on everything he needed to know.*

■■■■■■■■■■■■■■■■■■■■■■■■■■■■■■■■■■■■■■■■■■

*Damaris was at his house when he took out his phone and called his cousin Jared.*

*Jared: "Hey cousin, what's up man?"*

*Damaris: "Jared, we need you buddy."*

*Jared: "Everything okay bro?"*

*Damaris: "No bro, listen I need you to meet up with us tonight…"*

*Jared: "What do you mean?"*

*Damaris told him everything.*

*Jared: "Shit okay, I'll be there."*

■■■■■■■■■■■■■■■■■■■■■■■■■■■■■■■■■■■■■■■■■■■■■■■

*The Short Kid took out his phone and called The Cruiser.*

*The Cruiser: "Yo."*

*Short Kid: "Cruiser, we need your help! Can you drive us all to the city tonight?"*

*The Cruiser: "Sure man, I wasn't doing anything tonight anyway."*

*Short Kid: "Great, meet us tonight at The Author's house!"*

■■■■■■■■■■■■■■■■■■■■■■■■■■■■■■■■■■■■■■■■■■■■■■■

*Nighttime arrived, and the entire crew was at The Author's house, ready for battle.*

*Author: "Alright, the whole gang is here!"*

*Damaris: "Yeah we sure are."*

*Randy noticed Damaris, so he decided to approach him.*

*Randy: "Commander, it's great to see you."*

*Damaris chuckled.*

*Damaris: "Commander? That's what my girlfriend calls me in the bedroom."*

*Author: "Alright, alright, that's enough."*

*Riley approached The Author.*

*Riley: "Hey Author, are you ready?"*

*Author: "I am!"*

*Marcus chimed in.*

*Marcus: "When I see his troops, I will crush their skulls!"*

*Jared and Short Kid were sitting on the couch drinking juice boxes listening to everyone else talk.*

*The Cruiser: "Trust me gang, Murphy won't win this."*

*They heard a knock at the door. The Author walked over to the door and opened it. It was The PyroManiac.*

*Author: "I'm glad you made it."*

*Pyro walks in with his hands in his jacket pockets. Natasha came over to Pyro and waved at him.*

*Natasha: "Hi, I'm a big fan!"*

*Short Kid: "Me too Nat, he's so cool!"*

*While they were geeking out, The Author's mom, dad, and brother came out to the living room and saw all 10 of these people.*

*Author's Dad: "Oh, I didn't know you were having company?"*

*Author's Mom: "Do your friends want snacks?"*

*Marcus: "YES WE DO!"*

*His mom went into the kitchen and brought out orange slices for everybody. The Author's parents then left the living room and talked to each other in their bedroom.*

*Author's Mom: "What's been going on with him lately?"*

*Author's Dad: "No clue."*

*The Author's brother, Tony pointed out something unusual to him.*

*Tony: "Uh, Author, is that that superhero dude from the news standing over there?"*

*He pointed over at The PyroManiac.*

*Author: "Uh, yeah we're just hanging out."*

*Tony: "Okay then?"*

*He then walked away and went into his room.*

*Randy: "Okay Author, is this everybody?"*

*Author: "Yes."*

*He stood in the middle of the room and busted out a giant chalk board.*

*Short Kid: "Bro, where did you get a big ass chalk board like that?"*

*Everyone laughed except Pyro and Randy.*

*Author: "Listen up everybody, here's the plan!"*

*The Author went to grab the chalk to draw on the board, but he couldn't find it.*

*Author: "Where's my chalk?"*

*Marcus: "This dude."*

*The Author let out a big sigh.*

*Author: "Alright, forget the chalk board, listen up..."*

*Everyone was paying attention.*

*Author: "We have three main objectives, rescue Ms. Garcia, stop Murphy's plan from coming to fruition, and most importantly, don't die."*

*Riley: "Sounds easy enough."*

*Damaris: "Trust me Riley, his goons are stronger and more powerful than you can imagine."*

*Author: "Yes that's true, but we literally have a time traveler with crazy technology, and a fire-resistant superhero on our side."*

*PyroManiac: "Mhm."*

*Randy: "We will win this!"*

*Jared finished his juice box and chimed in.*

*Jared: "This is so cool, we're like a cool ass team you see in superhero movies!"*

*Damaris: "Yeah, we sure are."*

*Jared looked over at The Author and asked him a question.*

*Jared: "So like what's our group name going to be?"*

*Short Kid: "How about we call ourselves, The Crime Fighting Teens?"*

*The PyroManiac: "Wow."*

*Natasha: "Yeah, that's sucks."*

*Riley: "What about The Unbreakable Gang?"*

*Marcus: "Lame!"*

*The Author thought about it, and it clicked in his head.*

*The Author: "I got it."*

*Everyone looked over at him.*

*The Author: "How about… The Resistance?"*

*Everyone thought about it for a second.*

*Riley: "The Resistance, yeah, I like it."*

*Jared: "Has a nice ring to it."*

*Randy stood there feeling a bit emotional as he thought about his friends from the future with the same name.*

*Randy: "I like it."*

*Author: "Alright then, let's go save the world."*

Aiden Branss

# MEANWHILE IN THE FUTURE

*For days, Murphy and his team were trying to figure out a way to recreate the device that sent Randy back in time. It was 10 at night, and the tensions were high.*

*Future Murphy: "DAMN IT!"*

*He slammed his fist into a table, and it broke in half! His troops standing nearby were frightened by his superhuman strength.*

*Future Murphy: "Why did they have my device?!"*

*He picked up a bottle of liquor from his bar and threw it against the wall!*

*Future Murphy: "WHAT DO THEY HAVE PLANNED?"*

*His wife Cynthia walked fast into his office with a pile of papers in her hand.*

*Cynthia: "Honey, the lab ran some test, and we've figured out where that Resistance member traveled to!"*

*Future Murphy: "Really, where did he go?"*

*He snatched the papers out of her hands and read the report...*

*Future Murphy: "So, he traveled back 30 years."*

*He threw the papers on the ground.*

*Future Murphy: "So, this is an attempt to alter the past..."*

*Cynthia: "Yes, they want to prevent your plan from success."*

*Future Murphy: "Shit."*

*Cynthia: "You should have finished reading those papers you threw on the floor."*

*Future Murphy: "Why?"*

*Cynthia: "Honey, the lab was able to recreate the time travel machine!"*

*Murphy was filled with excitement!*

*Future Murphy: "PERFECT!"*

*Cynthia: "It's stronger and more powerful than the original... it can send our entire army throughout any point in time."*

*He smiled.*

*Future Murphy: "That's amazing..."*

*He walked towards the window and began looking out...*

*Future Murphy: "Cynthia, they will try to change the past and prevent the invasion, we must stop them before it's to late."*

*He took a sip of water.*

*Future Murphy: "Prepare our entire army to travel back in time 30 years, we must begin the true invasion earlier!"*

*Outside his window were all of his tanks, jets, and troops preparing for battle.*

*Murphy: "Tell the troops to be ready in a few hours. Tonight, we shall change history!"*

*Cynthia: "Yes, let's give those kids a surprise..."*

BACK IN PRESENT dAY

*It was almost midnight, and the crew was still at The Author's house.*

*Author: "Okay, is everyone ready?"*

*Damaris: "Almost bro."*

*They all gathered their weapons and protective gear. Most of the crew was wearing black pants and black hoodies while The PyroManiac and Randy had on their usual attire. The Author was wearing black and blue basketball shoes, black dress pants, a white button up polo shirt with a blue blazer on over.*

*Riley: "Damn look at you!"*

*They had knives, guns, pepper spray, shields, body armor, blasters, first aid kits, and more.*

*Randy: "I knew it'd be a good idea to steal all of this crap from the police station."*

*Everyone in the crew each had enough to protect themselves.*

*Jared: "I'm ready."*

*Short Kid: "Let's go get this dickhead."*

*Author: "Let's do this!"*

*As they were all about to head out to the front door to get in The Cruiser's car, Randy said something that The Author didn't like.*

*Randy: "When I see Murphy, I swear, I will kill him for everything he's done..."*

*The Author stopped walking and turned around to face him.*

*Author: "Okay, we're not doing that."*

*Randy: "What do you mean we're not killing him?"*

*Author: "I've known that dude for years, so we're not going to do that."*

*Randy was puzzled.*

*Randy: "What the hell are you talking about?!"*

*He walked up closer to The Author.*

*Randy: "He needs to be stopped!"*

*Author: "But killing him isn't the answer!"*

*The tension was felt throughout the entire room.*

*Randy: "You know what... I was wrong about you."*

*Author: "We are doing this my way, whether you like it or not!"*

*Randy was getting unbelievably mad.*

*Randy: "Move out of my way Author, I'm doing this my way..."*

*Author: "NO!"*

*Randy: "Fine, I'll make you move."*

*He turned on his jetpack and headed straight towards The Author!*

*Author: "WHAT THE- !"*

*He flew into The Author and rammed him into the wall!*

*Randy: "I'm sorry I had to do that but stay out of my way!"*

*The Author took pepper spray out of his pocket and sprayed it right in Randy's eyes!*

*Randy: "AHH!"*

*He took a swing at The Author and hit him right in the jaw!*

*Author: "YOU FUCKER!"*

*He tackled Randy to the ground and knocked his head into the floor when he took him down!*

*Riley: "STOP FIGHTING!"*

*Randy turned on his jetpack, picked up The Author and threw him right into his TV!*

*Short Kid: "STOP!"*

*The Cruiser and Marcus were sitting on the couch eating popcorn enjoying the show. Damaris looked over at PyroManiac.*

*Damaris: "Dude stop them!"*

*The Author got up and was in pain, when he saw his television was destroyed!*

*Author: "You broke my fucking TV!"*

*He jumped up and grabbed Randy's ankle and pulled him down onto the ground! He then jumped on top of him, grabbed him by the neck and started to strangle Randy!*

*Natasha: "Author stop it!!!"*

*Riley: "BABE STOP IT!"*

*Randy face was turning red and he couldn't breathe! He began scratching at The Author's face!*

*PyroManiac: "THAT'S ENOUGH!"*

*He ran up to The Author and forcibly pulled him off Randy. He picked up Randy and pushed him backed against a wall with his forearm across Randy's neck. Randy started coughing and catching his breath. The entire crew was shocked by what they all just saw. The Author was full of rage! After a moment Randy finally caught his breath.*

*Randy: "I didn't want to say it, but you leave me no choice!"*

*Author: "What do you mean by that?!"*

*Randy: "Do you really wanna know what happens in the future, HUH?!"*

*Everyone was paying close attention.*

*Randy: "YOU, AND ALL YOUR FRIENDS, DIE, AT THE HANDS OF MURPHY!"*

*Everyone was shocked and The Author became full of fear.*

*Randy: "You all fucking die, the invasion is successful, and Murphy rules the world!"*

*Author: "Oh my god..."*

*Randy: "We need to stop him, or everyone you know and love is going to die!"*

*The Author froze for a moment. He didn't know what to think.*

*Author: "Randy, I didn't know..."*

*Randy: "I'm sorry for fighting you, but please, I've already lost everyone once, I don't want to lose everyone again. My time travel device broke when I arrived here, so I don't get any redoes. This is our only chance to stop him. After tonight, it's too late."*

*The Author: "Randy, let me try to fix this first... if not, you can do whatever you want..."*

*The Author got a bit emotional in his voice.*

*The Author: "Please, he's been my best friend for my whole life, and I don't want to lose him."*

*A few tears came down his face.*

*Randy: "Okay Author, you got a deal."*

*Pyro let go of him.*

*Randy: "The Resistance will win today."*

*Author: "Yes we will!"*

*They all headed outside and went to the car. The Cruiser hopped in the driver seat, and Randy and PyroManiac were preparing to fly over to the city! The rest of the gang all crammed into the SUV.*

*The Cruiser: "Is everyone ready?"*

*Damaris: "Yep we're all good in here!"*

*Randy: "I'm ready for takeoff, we'll meet you guys there!"*

*He turned over and looked over at Pyro.*

*Randy: "You ready?"*

*PyroManiac: "I was born ready!"*

*They both flew up into the air and began to fly over to Theodore Tower, and The Cruiser started the car and sped off!*

*Author: "Tonight, our lives will change forever..."*

■■■■■■■■■■■■■■■■■■■■■■■■■■■■■■■■■■■■■■■■■■■■■

*Murphy was sitting in his office with no lights on when one of his troops came in.*

*"Sir, those mafia guys will be here soon to purchase the buildings."*

*Murphy: "Perfect, I cannot wait for our true plan to begin. I just need to get this out of the way first."*

*The troop walked out of the room, and Murphy leaned back in his chair and lit a cigar.*

*Murphy: "Tonight, my life will change forever."*

■■■■■■■■■■■■■■■■■■■■■■■■■■■■■■■■■■■■■■■■■■■■

*Ms. Garcia was sitting in the room still handcuffed. It has been over 24 hours that she's been imprisoned. She constantly kept hearing the troops walking past her door gossiping.*

*"You ready for tonight?"*

*"YES, I can't wait for the invasion to begin!"*

*Ms. Garcia sat there sad and felt hopeless.*

*Ms. Garcia: "It seems like tonight everything will change forever."*

158

••••••••••••••••••••••••••••••••••••••••••••

*Gwen, the mother living in the shelter in town, heard rumors of the shelter shutting down in just a few short hours. Her kids were sleeping, and she couldn't rest. She was worried about what she was going to do if the shelter did close down. She thought to herself "Tonight, everything will change for my family." She then looked at her kids and began to cry, and she worried what was next to come.*

••••••••••••••••••••••••••••••••••••••••••••

*Back in the future, Cynthia told Murphy some news.*

*Cynthia: "Hey, the army is ready to go back in time!"*

*Future Murphy: "Great, tonight, our lives shall change forever as we begin the invasion earlier than I originally did."*

••••••••••••••••••••••••••••••••••••••••••••

*Author: "Tonight..."*

••••••••••••••••••••••••••••••••••••••••••••

*Murphy: "Tonight..."*

••••••••••••••••••••••••••••••••••••••••••••

*Ms. Garcia "Tonight..."*

••••••••••••••••••••••••••••••••••••••••••••

*Gwen: "Tonight..."*

••••••••••••••••••••••••••••••••••••••••••••

***Future Murphy: "Tonight..."***

FRidAY

*Anxiety.*
*Guilt.*
*Anger.*
*Fear.*

*These were the emotions running through The Author's head. His eyes were closed the entire ride to the city. His palms were sweaty, and he did his best to control his breathing. His anxiety was at an all-time high! He also just had a bad feeling in his stomach. Just a few days ago, he was ditching school with Murphy, and everything was fine. Now a few short days later, he was going to war with him, for the fate of the entire world! The Author kept thinking about Mr. Theodore, the great man who always wanted to help people. Now, his teenage grandson wants to do the exact opposite and hurt people. He felt guilty, he wished he had insisted that Mr. Theodore should have taken his heart medication, so he'd still be alive. He wished things could have been different.*
*He began to repeat this all in his head, and the more he thought about it all, the angrier he got. He thought to himself "What the fuck is wrong with Murphy?! He's lost his damn mind!" And the more he thought about it the more he was getting pissed off! He wanted to smack some sense into this kid! He eventually opened his eyes, and he looked around the car. His girlfriend Riley was sleeping and was leaning her head against the window. Natasha was next to her biting her nails. The Cruiser was silent, paying attention to the road. Damaris was in the passenger seat praying. In the back, The Short Kid was hitting his vape, while Marcus was lifting a dumbbell.*

*Jared was looking out the window watching Pyro and Randy zooming through the sky. The two men flying were silent as well.*
*Then it truly began to set in. The Author felt an immense amount of fear. The fear of his friends getting hurt, the fear of losing, and the fear of death all set in. The Author was panicking in silence.*

■■■■■■■■■■■■■■■■■■■■■■■■■■■■■■■■■■■■■■■■■■■■

*Murphy watched the clock move every second, he could not wait until the men arrived so he could begin the invasion he'd always dreamt about!*

*Murphy: "I can't believe this is real life..."*

*The severity of his actions began to slowly come upon him, and for a moment he began to second guess himself, until a troop came into his office.*

*"Sir, that man Tony Ravioli and his crew will be here shortly."*

*Murphy: "Fantastic."*

■■■■■■■■■■■■■■■■■■■■■■■■■■■■■■■■■■■■■■■■■■■

*The Author finally heard the words he was dreading to hear the entire car ride.*

*The Cruiser: "We're almost there."*

*They were about 2 blocks away.*

*Author: "Cruiser, just park right up here on the corner."*

*The Cruiser: "You sure?"*

*Author: "Yeah."*

*He pulled the car over and the entire crew hopped out the car.*

*Author: "Cruiser, stay here with the whip and keep an eye out."*

*The Cruiser: "Got it."*

*The Author turned around and looked at his crew.*

*Author: "Resistance, are we ready!?"*

*Damaris: "You know it!"*

*Short Kid: "Fuck yeah!"*

*Riley: "Let's do this!"*

*They each had an earpiece in so they could talk to one another. The Author called for two members over their communicators.*

*Author: "Randy and Pyro, how's it look up there?"*

*The two of them were flying around the building keeping an eye out.*

*PyroManiac: "I'm looking through the windows on each floor of the tower, I see a few of his troops, but no sight of Murphy."*

*Author: "Okay, Randy, do you copy?"*

*Randy: "Yes, I have eyes on something…"*

*A black limo was pulling up to Theodore Tower, the windows were tinted, and Randy couldn't see who it was inside.*

*Randy: "There's a limo pulling up."*

*The limo stopped right outside the building, and multiple men in suits were getting out the car.*

*"Let's hurry up and get this over with boss."*

*Author: "Those are probably the people who are going to buy the buildings."*

*Natasha chimed in.*

*Natasha: "What should we do about them?"*

*Author: "Pyro, Randy, one of you take them out, but quietly, we need to do this stealthy."*

*The Author stopped talking to them and looked over at the crew.*

*Author: "Come on everyone, let's move!"*

*They all began running towards the skyscraper! PyroManiac and Randy were up in the sky staring down at the mob guys.*

*PyroManiac: "You wanna get them?"*

*Randy: "I got an idea, let's take them out one by one without any of them noticing."*

*They slowly flew down and landed before any of the 4 mob guys saw them. When PyroManiac and Randy landed on the ground, their shoes made a small thumping sound when they hit the pavement.*

*"Did y'all hear something?"*

*"Forget about it, let's head in."*

*The men all walked in a straight line. The man in the back dragged behind a bit, and it gave Randy the perfect opportunity to swoop in, hit him in the head and knock him out! He pulled his unconscious body off to the side. Then PyroManiac jumped up in the air and grabbed two of the men and threw them to both into the ground before they could make any noise!*

*"You guys ready for this? Uh... guys?"*

*He turned around and saw his men were nowhere in sight!*

*"WHAT THE-!"*

*Before he finished his sentence, Randy came up from behind him and hit the guy in the head with his blaster sending him onto the ground unconscious!*

*Randy: "Got 'em!"*

*The Author and the crew ran up to the building.*

*Author: "Did you get those guys?"*

*Randy: "We did!"*

*Damaris and Short Kid were huffing and puffing, they were completely out of breath!*

*Damaris: "Woah! I thought it'd be easier to run 2 blocks!"*

*Short Kid: \*Wheezing\**

*Short Kid: "For real bro."*

*Marcus: "Y'all really need to hit the gym."*

*Jared: "Respectfully Marcus, shut up."*

*Marcus: "Whatever sissy..."*

*Jared: "Hey shut the hell up!"*

*Marcus: "MAKE ME!"*

*Natasha: "GROW UP YOU TWO!"*

*The PyroManiac stomped his foot on the ground and yelled in a demonic voice as his aura glowed a bit.*

*PyroManiac: "ENOUGH!"*

*They all shut up.*

*Author: "Listen to me everyone, we need to stay united!"*

*Riley: "He's right, tell us your plan."*

*The Author stood firm when he looked up straight at the building. He couldn't even see the top of the building as it was hidden in the foggy sky.*

*Author: "Okay listen up everyone, have your weapons at your side!"*

*Everyone took out their weapons when he said that.*

*Author: "We need to split up… Randy, Marcus, Jared, and Natasha, I need you 4 to find and rescue Ms. Garcia."*

*Natasha: "You got it."*

*Damaris: "What about the rest of us?"*

*Author: "I'm going to get into that. Me, Pyro, Damaris, Short Kid and Riley, are going to find Murphy, we'll most likely have to fight through his troops, but Pyro will take care of most of them."*

*Short Kid: "What do we do once we find him?"*

*Author: "Cover my back, and I'll see what I can do."*

*They all prepared themselves and took deep breaths.*

*Author: "Y'all ready?"*

*They all shouted "YES!"*

*Author: "Alright let's do this!"*

*They all had their weapons ready, and they all ran inside the building. They walked in the entrance, and it was still pitch black in there!*

*Damaris: "Damn it, it's still dark in here!"*

*Author: "Lower your voice a bit, this is a good thing, we can sneak in here without anyone noticing."*

*Damaris: "Oh yeah true."*

*They ran over to where the stairs and elevator were, and the gang kept their movements as silent as possible.*

*Author: "Okay let's split up, me and my crew, let's head up the stairs to the 29th floor..."*

*Randy: "But wait Author, where are they keeping Linda captured?"*

*Author: "I don't know, but I'm sure you'll figure it out, but let's move!"*

*So, The Author, The PyroManiac, Damaris, Riley, and The Short Kid all ran up the stairs to get to Murphy's office!*

*Short Kid: "FUCK I HATE THESE STAIRS!"*

*Randy went to the elevator and called over Marcus, Jared and Natasha and they waited for the door to open, and once it did, they all got in.*

*Jared: "So like, where are we even going?"*

*Randy clicked 10th floor button for no reason.*

*Marcus: "Why that floor?"*

*Randy: "I have an idea..."*

*They arrived on the 10th floor and the four of them all hid behind a wall. Nearby there was one of Murphy's troops standing around. Randy ducted and slowly walked behind the man. He got close up to him, moved fast, and then he pointed his blaster directly in the troops back!*

*Randy: "If you want to live, you'll tell me where you have a woman named Linda Garcia captive!"*

*"OKAY OKAY PLEASE DON'T SHOOT, I'LL TAKE YOU THERE, SHE'S ON THE 60th FLOOR!"*

*Randy: "Great, now move!"*

*The troop walked them to the elevator and went all the way up with them to the 60th floor! Once they arrived up there, he walked them to the room where she was being held. Marcus snatched the keys to the room off the troops belt clip. They unlocked the door and saw Ms. Garcia sitting in there chained up to a pole while lying on the floor.*

*Natasha: "Oh my…"*

*Randy ran up to her and tore off her handcuffs! She looked at him, and she was very tired, hungry and scared.*

*Ms. Garcia: "Aren't you that guy I punched at the event?"*

*Randy: "Yeah… I'll explain everything later."*

*She stood up on her own, and Natasha gave her some water and granola bars. She chowed it all down in just a few seconds and felt immediately better. Meanwhile, the other crew was running up the stairs and they were dying!*

*Riley: "OH MY GOD I HATE THESE STAIRS!"*

*Short Kid: \*Wheeze\**

*Damaris: "This sucks."*

*Even The Author was sweating a bit.*

*Author: "Damn we really should have taken the elevator!"*

*The PyroManiac made it up the stairs fast and got to the $29^{th}$ floor. He looked through the window in the door and saw that the entire floor was filled with armed troops!*

*PyroManiac: "Room at least got 30 troops in here."*

*Once the rest of them caught up with Pyro, and caught their breath, they tried to think of what to do next.*

*Riley: "Is there a way we could sneak in?"*

*Author: "Probably not, the only way in and out to this floor is through this door, or the elevator."*

*PyroManiac: "I'm goin' in."*

*Author: "Lead the way, and I'll get Murphy!"*

*In his office, Murphy was sitting at his desk with one of his troops.*

*Murphy: "Where are these dudes at? It's way past 2 AM! I can't begin the invasion till I get the money!"*

*Then all of a sudden PyroManiac kicked down the door and caught the attention of all the troops on the floor, and Murphy heard it from his office.*

*Murphy: "What the hell was that?"*

*Pyro rushed in and started to attack all the troops! He ran up to one of them, punched him in the gut, and threw him across the room knocking down other troops in the process! Murphy opened the door of his office and saw the chaos happening!*

*Murphy: "What the hell!"*

*Author: "MURPHY!"*

*Murphy: "Oh shit."*

*Murphy turned back in his office and started running! The Author chased after him while Pyro was still taking out this room full of troops! The Author ran into Murphy's office when he didn't see him anywhere in sight. The troop that was in the room snuck up and grabbed Author from behind!*

*Author: "DAMN IT!"*

*The Author quickly took out a pair of brass knuckles from his pocket, put his fingers through the holes, and socked the guy right in the face! The troop fell to the ground unconscious, and The Author noticed a hidden door that was open, and it sounded like footsteps running upwards.*

*Author: "MURPHY GET BACK HERE!"*

*The Author went towards the door, but something on Murphy's desk caught his attention. He walked to the desk and saw that there was a blunt just sitting there. Murphy was going to smoke it at some point, and without thinking too much about it The Author took it and put it in a pocket in his blazer. He then ran towards the door and saw Murphy running up the stairs as fast as he can.*

*Author: "Really, you're going to run up this emergency staircase to avoid me?!"*

*Murphy: "SCREW YOU AUTHOR!"*

*He kept running up the stairs and grabbed his walkie-talkie to send a message out to all his troops!*

*Murphy: "THE BUILDING HAS BEEN COMPROMISED, LOCK ALL THE DOORS, CAPTURE THE INTRUDERS!"*

*The Author started running up the stairs and began chasing after him.*

*Author: "COME HERE!"*

*Murphy: "You'll never catch me!"*

*Meanwhile upstairs, Randy and that crew were on their way back downstairs.*

*Ms. Garcia: "Thank you for saving me."*

*Randy: "Don't mention it, luckily for us we did this without being caught."*

*Then the lights in the entire building turned red, and then a super loud alarm noise started to blast!*

*"INTRUDER ALERT! INTRUDER ALERT!"*

*Jared: "Ah shit."*

*Natasha: "I bet 5 bucks The Author did this."*

*Randy: "LET'S MOVE!"*

*They ran over to the elevator, but it wouldn't open!*

*Randy: "DAMN IT!"*

*Ms. Garcia: "Why's it not opening?!"*

*Randy: "They've must have turned it off!"*

*Marcus: "Hold up."*

*Marcus walked towards the elevator buttons and strutted with his big beefy arms dangling down.*

*Marcus: "I got this."*

*Marcus took his arm back, got his form ready, and PUNCHED the elevator buttons, destroying the button panel, and his hand began to bleed!*

*Ms. Garcia: "WHAT DID YOU DO THAT FOR!?"*

*Marcus: "Crap, that usually works in movies."*

*Natasha: "Fucking dumbass."*

*Jared: "Whatever let's get to the stairs!"*

*Randy: "Good thinking kid!"*

*Then the 5 of them all ran over to the staircase on the other side of the floor, but before they could make it, they were suddenly stopped by a mob of troops that pointed their guns at them!*

*"FREEZE!"*

*"DON'T MOVE!"*

*Randy: "Crap!"*

*Meanwhile downstairs, PyroManiac, Riley, Damaris and Short Kid were fighting off the remaining troops! A troop tried to grab Riley, and she took out her pepper spray!*

*Riley: "Tell me how this taste?"*

*She then sprayed it all in their face!*

*"AHHHHHHHHH!"*

*Damaris was running around the room avoiding the attacks from the troops! He was using a taser to zap all of them to distract them, while Short Kid would come from behind them and shove them to the ground!*

*Short Kid: "Haha got you bitch."*

*They did this to about 5 troops until one of them grabbed Short Kid by the neck! He began to choke him! PyroManiac noticed this and flew over and knocked him off! He kicked the man's forehead, then grabbed the man's hand, and with only a bit of his strength, he broke every bone in his hand!*

*"STOP PLEASE!"*

*Pyro let go but not before he slammed the trooper's body into the floor! Riley came up from the other side and spit on the man.*

*Riley: "How pathetic, you really hurt a little boy!"*

*Damaris got the last trooper in the room, and they fell to the ground.*

*Damaris: "Was that all of them?"*

*Meanwhile, The Author was still chasing Murphy up the stairs! He had run all the way up to the $70^{th}$ floor, but Murphy was ahead of him a bit. The Author could hear Murphy's voice echo through the entire staircase.*

*Murphy: "Feeling tired yet?"*

*Author: "Not a bit!"*

*Truthfully, he was super exhausted running up all these steps, but he wasn't going to give up!*

*Author: "GET DOWN HERE!"*

*And he kept chasing him up! Back on the $60^{th}$ floor, the crew was stuck in a bad situation.*

*"Put your hands up in the air if you want to live!"*

*Natasha: "What do we do?!"*

*Randy: "There's nothing we can do..."*

*He put his hands up, and the crew was shocked.*

*Randy: "Ha, just kidding."*

*He reached in his pocket and whipped out a grenade!*

*Ms. Garcia: "WHAT THE!"*

*The troops were shivering in their boots.*

*Randy: "Listen you filthy troops..."*

*He put his finger on the safety pin.*

*Randy: "I will pull this little pin right off, and it'll kill us all!"*

*Marcus: "Okay, this dude is crazy!"*

*Randy: "So listen up, this is going to go one of two ways, you're going to let us go to those stairs, or, you'll all get blown up, so think wisely."*

*"Uh..."*

*"What the fuck..."*

*"What do we do?"*

*The troops were scared, they wanted to obey Murphy, but they didn't want to die.*

*"Okay, let them through, we don't get paid enough for this."*

*The troops put down their weapons and moved out the way to let the crew get to the doorway. They ran towards and opened the door to the staircase.*

*Jared: "I can't believe that worked!"*

*Ms. Garcia: "You are a crazy man, but I thought it was charming!"*

*Randy: "Yeah, you can thank me for saving your lives later, but let's hurry up and meet with the rest of the crew!"*

*They all ran downstairs to the floor where the rest of the crew was. Meanwhile, The Author had chased Murphy all the way to the top floor of the skyscraper!*

*Author: "Give it up Murphy, there's nowhere else to run besides the roof!"*

*Murphy: "STOP FOLLOWING ME!"*

*Murphy got to the very top and opened the door that led right to the roof. The Author got up there too, and now they were both up on the roof, almost 100 stories high up in the sky! The Author looked up at the sky and saw that they were all the way up in the clouds!*

*Author: "Holy shit, this is way to high up!"*

*As he thought about how high up he was, he felt Murphy jump up from behind him, and he punched him in the back of the head!*

*Author: "AH FUCK!"*

*He composed himself right away and faced Murphy.*

*Author: "You don't want to do this."*

*Murphy: "But I do."*

*Author: "Fine."*

*The Author charged at Murphy and punched him in the face!*

*Murphy: "Your punches are weak."*

*Murphy tackled him to the ground, and they wrestled a bit.*

*Murphy: "Give it up Author!"*

*Author: "NO!"*

*The Author gained enough strength to throw Murphy off of him! They both stood up, but then Author grabbed Murphy by the head, pulled him down, and kneed him right in the face!*

*Murphy: "AH!"*

*Murphy punched The Author in the gut like how he did the other day!*

*Author: "Damn it!"*

*Murphy: "I just don't get it, why won't you quit?!"*

*The Author put on his brass knuckles and hit Murphy right in the face!*

*Murphy: "SHIT!"*

*He fell to the ground, and The Author kicked him in the stomach! Murphy was in pain!*

*Author: "You wanna know why I'm doing this?!"*

*He kicked him again!*

*Author: "BECAUSE YOU ARE ACTING LIKE A FUCKING IDIOT!"*

*He kicked him again!*

*Murphy: "Stop it!"*

*Author: "NO! YOU NEED TO STOP!"*

*He kicked him again for the fourth time! At this point it seemed like Murphy was done.*

*Author: "Your grandpa would be so ashamed of you."*

*Murphy: "What do you even mean?"*

*Author: "What do I mean?! I mean that he was a great man who did a lot of good things for people, and you wanna do the exact opposite!"*

*Murphy: "You just don't get it..."*

*Author: "I DO GET IT! You think you can rule the world with that money! You wanna act like a big bad guy, but really, you are just a stupid kid with an ego!"*

*Murphy: "You are wrong! You don't know me like that!"*

*Author: "But I do, we've been best friends our whole lives!"*

*Murphy started to deeply think about everything, and suddenly he started to feel a bit of grief and regret.*

*Author: "If you do this, you will ruin all the good that is associated with your family name! Do you really want your legacy to be that you were known as Murphy, the evil terrible man?!"*

*Murphy started to let out a few tears but hid it from The Author.*

*Author: "Don't let your life story become known as the legend of Evil Murphy..."*

*Murphy looked up, and the reality of everything set in...*

*Murphy: "Oh my god... what am I doing, what am I thinking?"*

*He got up a bit and the tears began to run down his face. He let out a scream of raw anger and grief as he thought about his grandfather. The emotion was taking him over.*

*Murphy: "I'm sorry Author, you're right..."*

*Author was a bit surprised.*

*Author: "You can end this all right here, right now."*

*Murphy slowly stood back up and looked over the edge of the building.*

*Murphy: "You're right, I can end it all."*

*He walked towards the edge of the building and stared all the way down the skyscraper. He couldn't even see the street down below.*

*Murphy: "I'm sorry for everything."*

*Author realized what Murphy was about to do!*

*Author: "WAIT I DIDN'T MEAN END IT LIKE THAT!!!"*

*He ran up to Murphy to try to calm down the situation!*

*Murphy: "Don't come any closer, or I'll jump!"*

*Author: "PLEASE DON'T MURPHY!!"*

*He put his hand out to him in a calm manner.*

*Author: "Please just come away from the edge."*

*Murphy looked down at the ground and didn't know what to think.*

*Murphy: "I fucked up, I can't ever be forgiven for what I've done."*

*Author: "Yes you can bro, if you end all this nonsense, I will forgive you."*

*Murphy: "I just…"*

*Author: "Please bro, I don't want to lose my best friend."*

*Murphy thought for a moment and took in The Author's words.*

*Murphy: "Okay, I'll move."*

*What happened next, The Author saw in slow motion… As Murphy turned around to face The Author, he was about to take a step forward when he began to slip backwards. They both had terrified looks on their faces! Murphy was about to fall off the building, when The Author jumped down right on his stomach, reached out his hand, and caught Murphy before it was too late!*

*Murphy: "HOLY SHIT!"*

*Murphy was dangling off the skyscraper! He was staring straight down at his fate! The only thing keeping him alive was The Author's grip on him!*

*Author: "HOLD ON I'LL PULL YOU UP!"*

*He tried pulling up Murphy, but he was super heavy. Then, The Author began to slowly slip off the building…*

*Murphy: "AUTHOR YOUR SLIPPING!"*

*Author: "SHIT!"*

*Murphy: "LET GO OF ME OR ELSE YOUR GONNA FALL!"*

*Author: "NO!"*

*The Author kept trying to pull him up but with no luck and he kept slowly slipping off the edge more!*

*Murphy: "LET GO!"*

*Author: "NO I WON'T!"*

*He kept slowly slipping off the building, and the end was near for both of them. In this moment, The Author looked at Murphy in his eyes, and he began to have flashbacks of when they were kids. He thought about times they went to the park, times they went out to eat, times they'd play video games together, and times they hung out after school. The Author thought of a time they'd biked in the snow and thought of another time the year prior to this when they fought a kid who tried to stab The Author in the eye! All the memories they shared flashed before his eyes in less than a second.*
*When the flashbacks ended, The Author was set back in the reality of the situation. His body was almost about to fall off the building if he slid forward one more inch! He looked at Murphy, and in that moment, he gained a boost of strength and confidence! With all of his might, The Author pulled up as hard as he could! He used all of his strength to pick up Murphy! He moved his body back away*

*from the edge and lifted up Murphy with everything he had! He struggled and tore a few muscles. Murphy slowly was pulled up by him, and The Author stood up, and used one last boost of strength to get Murphy up! With all his force, he pulled up as hard as he could, and got Murphy back up on the roof of the skyscraper! The boys were both catching their breath after that near death experience and were both in shock. Murphy looked over at The Author, surprised.*

*Murphy: "Author, you just, you saved my life..."*

*Author was still trying to calm himself down.*

*Murphy: "I don't get it, after everything I've done, you still risked your life for mine. Why?"*

*Author: "Because Murphy, you always have to do what's right, even if it hurts."*

*Murphy: "What do you mean?"*

*Author: "It's an expression my parents always told me. It basically means you need to always do what's morally right, even if it can be bad, or hurt you in the end."*

*Murphy: "Author, thank you..."*

*The boys began to both cry a bit, and they both hugged each other.*

*Murphy: "Thank you for not giving up on me."*

*He stepped back, and Murphy grabbed his walkie-talkie and sent out a message.*

*Murphy: "Troops, stand down, and go home."*

*He then threw his walkie-talkie off the roof.*

*Murphy: "I'm not selling the buildings, and from this moment on, I promise I will continue the legacy of my grandfather."*

*Author: "That's great Murphy, let's go downstairs and meet with my crew."*

*Murphy: "Alright Author."*

*So then, the two friends walked down all the stairs they had just ran up, and they slowly walked down to the floor where Murphy's office was. They opened the door to the floor, and the entire crew was waiting there for him. They all turned their attention over to them when they saw Murphy was there.*

*Author: "Resistance, we won."*

*PyroManiac: "Huh?"*

*Author: "Yep."*

*Randy walked up towards The Author.*

*Randy: "I gotta say, I'm impressed your plan worked."*

*Riley: "So wait, did we save the world?"*

*Author: "Yeah, I guess we did!"*

*Murphy stepped in the conversation.*

*Murphy: "Everyone, I know your all here because of me, and I'd like to say I'm sorry for everything…"*

*Damaris: "Well you did try to kill us the other day, but I guess I can forgive."*

*Short Kid: "Yeah, me too."*

*The Author smiled.*

*Author: "Let's get ready to go home…"*

*The Cruiser was chilling in his SUV listening to some tunes and singing along by himself.*

*The Cruiser: "YOU! YOU GOT WHAT I NEED! BUT YOU SAY HE'S JUST A FRIEND, BUT YOU SAY HE'S JUST A FRIEND!"*

*He turned down the volume on his car radio and sat back a bit.*

*The Cruiser: "Man I love this song! I wonder how everything is going in there?"*

*He busted out an energy drink and began chugging it. Suddenly he saw something odd, something extremely strange in his rear-view mirror. It was unlike anything he had ever seen before…*

*The Cruiser: "HOLY SHIT!"*

*Back in the building, everyone's communicator went off, and The Cruiser was screaming!*

*The Cruiser: "GUYS SOMETHING CRAZY IS GOING ON HELP—!"*

*Their communicators began to fizzle out and all everyone heard was static!*

*Author: "What the hell..."*

*Randy: "Murphy, what did you do?"*

*Murphy: "I promise I didn't do anything!"*

*They looked out the window of his office, and weird balls of light began forming in the sky.*

*Riley: "What's going on?!"*

*Natasha: "I'm starting to get scared!"*

*The crew had no idea what was going on! Until all of those bright balls in the sky became to grow and formed into giant circles! There were hundreds of them appearing out of nowhere in the sky and all throughout the city!*

*PyroManiac: "The fuck?"*

*Damaris: "No clue what's going on!"*

*The light circles became fully formed into giant portals! Suddenly, a fighter jet had come flying through one of the portals!*

*Short Kid: "WHAT THE FUCK!"*

*Randy: "Oh no…"*

*Randy stood closer to the window.*

*Ms. Garcia: "Randy, what's going on, what are those things!?"*

*Randy: "Those are time portals…"*

*Jared: "What does that mean?"*

*Randy realized what was happening…*

*Randy: "Oh my god, he's found us!"*

*One of those light circles randomly showed up in the office with them!*

*Author: "Who found us?!"*

*The light grew, and formed into a portal, and through the other side, they saw a foot peeking out!*

*Randy: "M…Murphy!"*

*The man walked out of the portal, and he had a menacing look on his face…*

*Murphy: "Is that me from the future?!"*

*Future Murphy grinned.*

*Future Murphy: "Well, well, well…"*

*The crew was frightened and confused with everything going on!*

*Future Murphy: "Hello Randy."*

*He took a look around at the room.*

*Future Murphy: "Wow, it looks like you assembled past versions of your dead friends."*

*Marcus: "Wow, so Randy really wasn't lying about being from the future!"*

*Randy: "You thought this whole time I was... forget it!"*

*Future Murphy: "It's a shame that my former self almost backed out of the plan, coward."*

*Murphy: "Hey fuck you!"*

*Future Murphy laughed it off.*

*Future Murphy: "The invasion shall begin now!"*

*The crew turned around and saw more portals opening up! Then tanks, armed troops, and jets, began to come out of the portals, and started to consume the streets of the city! The entire crew was shocked, and they had their jaws hit the ground! They all looked on in horror!*

*Author: "WHAT! NO!!!"*

*Future Murphy: "Can I get some back up in here?"*

*Two troops from the future walked into the office.*

*Future Murphy: "Take my former self and keep him somewhere safe, if he gets hurt, you know what will happen."*

*The troops came up to Murphy and grabbed him.*

*Murphy: "HEY LET ME GO!"*

*They dragged him out of the room!*

*Future Murphy: "This war, has officially began, and you won't be able to stop me!"*

*PyroManiac balled up his fists, and glowed orange, and The Author looked over at his friends!*

*Author: "DAMARIS, SHORT KID, RILEY, NAT, JARED, MARCUS, MS. GARCIA GET OUT OF HERE NOW!"*

*The crew all ran out! Future Murphy spoke to his army over a communication device.*

*Future Murphy: "Cynthia, handle the group of kids who are about to run out the building, I'll handle the 3 in here…"*

*Cynthia: "On it."*

*The PyroManiac jumped up at Murphy and punched him in the face as hard as he could! However, Future Murphy was barely fazed by his punch.*

*Future Murphy: "I expected more of a good punch from a superhero."*

*Future Murphy grabbed Pyro and threw him against the wall!*

*Future Murphy: "BRING IT ON!!!!!"*

*Randy flew right towards him and began trying to take him on. Randy took out his blaster and began to shoot at him! The shots hit him, but it barely affected him!*

*Future Murphy: "Randy, THOSE SHOTS ARE WEAK FOR A SUPERHUMAN LIKE ME!"*

*Randy: "Shit!"*

*Future Murphy ran towards Randy and grabbed him by the neck!*

*Future Murphy: "Time to kill you, just like how I killed your Resistance buddy!"*

*The Author came up from behind him, took out a knife from his pocket, and stabbed Future Murphy in his back!*

*Future Murphy: "DAMN!"*

*He dropped Randy, his face was super red, and he tried to regain his breath!*

*Future Murphy: "Looks like I have to kill you again, Author!"*

*He walked towards The Author, and Author stood firm with his knife and brass knuckles out feeling fearless! PyroManiac tackled Future Murphy to the ground and began punching him in the face with his fire fists! Future Murphy became infuriated by the pain, so with all his force he pushed Pyro off of him onto the ground. He stood up fast and stomped Pyro in the chest with his boot! The PyroManiac yelled out loud in pain! While this was happening, the rest of the crew was running downstairs to escape the building!*

*Damaris: "What the hell is going on?!?"*

*Ms. Garcia "WERE ABOUT TO DIE, THAT'S WHAT'S GOING ON!"*

*They got back down to the first floor and busted their way out the building, and when they got outside it was the scariest sight any of them had ever seen!*

*Riley: \*GASP\**

*Tanks were roaming the streets, and thousands of troops were on foot! Then without a warning, a jet zooming through the sky began firing down bullets at the crew!*

*Marcus: "RUN!"*

*The entire crew ran away from the shots! Meanwhile the two troops were taking Murphy away into a secure location!*

*"Come with us!"*

*Murphy: "LET ME GO YOU BASTARDS!"*

*They each had a tight grip on him, and he was struggling to escape! He noticed the one troop had a blaster on his belt buckle, so Murphy swiftly snatched it from him!*

*"HEY!"*

*Murphy shot the guy he stole the blaster from, and he fell to the ground. He quickly took down the other troop. He was now free.*

*Murphy: "I just can't believe this, my future self, what the fuck? This doesn't make any sense!"*

*His mind was racing for a moment until he came back to his senses.*

*Murphy: "Alright, I have to go help my friends!"*

*He began to run to go find the rest of The Resistance! Meanwhile during the fight with Future Murphy...*

*Randy: "Guys, on the count of three, let's all jump on him!"*

*Author: "1."*

*PyroManiac: "2."*

*Randy: "3!"*

*They all hopped onto him! Pyro kept hitting him in the face with his fire fists, while Author and Randy tried to hold him down! The Author used the knife repeatedly to try to weaken him, but this just made Future Murphy even more pissed off!*

*Future Murphy: "THAT'S IT!"*

*He grabbed Pyro and threw him off of him! He then used his arms to reach behind him to pull Author and Randy off of him!*

*Randy: "FUCK!"*

*He used his jet pack to escape Murphy's grip, and The Author stabbed him in the hand, and Future Murphy dropped him!*

*Future Murphy: "You're gonna pay for that!"*

*The Author stood back a bit while Pyro tried to take him on again. Randy came next him.*

*Author: "Damn it Randy, I'm getting tired."*

*Randy: "I know, but we need to stop him!"*

*Author: "But how?! We're not strong enough."*

*Future Murphy grabbed and threw Pyro onto the ground! He got on top of Pyro and began punching his mask as hard as he could! He kept repeatedly slamming his fist into him, and the more he did, PyroManiac's mask began to crack! This made Pyro increasingly furious! He then used all of his force to push Future Murphy off of him. Pyro stood up and tackled Murphy so hard down into the ground they broke through the floor! Both of them slammed down onto the floor below them!*

*Randy: "Holy shit!"*

*Author: "I gotta be honest that was pretty cool."*

*Randy: "Let's move!"*

*Randy grabbed The Author and had the jetpack fly them both down to the floor below them! Meanwhile, the crew was outside running for their lives! Bullets were flying over their heads!*

*Riley: "WE ARE GOING TO DIE OUT HERE!"*

*Natasha: "THERE IS NO ESCAPE!"*

*The gang was running past a tank, when it suddenly shot a cannon into a building nearby! That scared the shit out of them!*

*Marcus: "DAMN!"*

*They sprinted as fast as they could to escape the danger, when suddenly Future Murphy's wife Cynthia stopped in front of them.*

*Cynthia: "Hello, Resistance."*

*Riley: "Whoa who's this bitch?"*

*Suddenly, a ship in the sky appeared out of nowhere!*

*Ms. Garcia: "WHAT IS THAT?"*

*Cynthia laughed.*

*Cynthia: "A flying ship, what else would it be, and girl, I don't appreciate you calling me a bitch..."*

*She took out a communication device and spoke to the people in the giant flying ship above them!*

*Cynthia: "Send a beam down and lock up these fools!"*

*A giant beam projecting from the ship came down onto the streets and everyone jumped out of the way before it could touch them, except Damaris and Short Kid.*

*Short Kid: "What the hell is this?"*

*They couldn't escape the beam, and it started to pull them up in the air!*

*Damaris: "Woah are we levitating!?"*

*Cynthia: "Damn, it missed most of them, whatever beam up these two stupid looking boys."*

*Damaris: "Hey fuck you—!"*

*The beam levitated the two of them high up into the sky and abducted them! They were both screaming the entire time they were floating up towards the ship! Once they both reached the ship, they were both grabbed by one of Murphy's troops and pulled onto the ship!*

*"DON'T MOVE!"*

*Damaris: "Damn it!"*

*Back on the ground, the crew was facing off with Cynthia.*

*Cynthia: "It would have been nice if that damn beam would have taken you all onto the ship, whatever, looks like I'll just have to take you out myself!"*

*She reached into her back pocket and took out a blaster. She was getting ready to shoot the entire crew!*

*Jared: "Oh no..."*

*Meanwhile, the fight in Theodore Tower was getting intense! After The PyroManiac sent Future Murphy crashing through the floor, they each took a second to catch their breath!*

*PyroManiac: "Give up, you lost now."*

*Future Murphy: "Not a chance!"*

*Future Murphy stood up and charged at Pyro! Randy held The Author as they flew down to the floor.*

*Author: "Randy, drop me onto him!"*

*He put on his brass knuckles and had his knife ready in his other hand!*

*Randy: "You sure?"*

*Author: "Yes!"*

*Future Murphy was pounding in PyroManiac's face! He punched him so hard that the left glass eyepiece on his gas mask broke off, and his real eye was showing, and it was glowing orange with small flames in his pupils...*

*Future Murphy: "You are about to die fire boy!"*

*He raised his fist above PyroManiac's face and was about to paralyze this man! Until The Author dropped on top of him, and he shoved the knife deep into the back of his neck!*

*Future Murphy: "AHH!"*

*He used the brass knuckles and punched him in the face a few times! That's when Randy came swooping in and rammed Future Murphy into a wall! Then Pyro got up and held him against the wall while he punched and kicked him as hard as he could! They all had a good grip on him, and Future Murphy couldn't escape!*

*Author: "DON'T LET GO!"*

*Meanwhile, on the ship in the sky, Damaris and Short Kid were held at gun point by a troop after they had been beamed up onto the flying ship!*

*Short Kid: "LET US OFF THIS THING!"*

*"SHUT YOUR MOUTH, YOU SHORT IDIOT!"*

*For some reason, that REALLY set off his emotions...*

*Short Kid: "What did you just call me?"*

*"A SHORT IDIOT!"*

*He took a deep breath in and had given the troop a look that he had never given anyone before in his life.*

*Short Kid: "You messed with the wrong kid today..."*

*"What?"*

*Short Kid ran towards the troop and tackled him to the ground!*

*Short Kid: "DAMARIS HELP ME OUT YOU LAZY FUCK!"*

*Damaris: "Oh okay!"*

*Damaris ran over and helped Short Kid take out the troop! The troop had two blasters on them, so the boys each kept one for themselves.*

*Damaris: "Okay now what?"*

*More troops entered the room and began to open fire!*

*Short Kid: "GET DOWN!"*

*They both crouched down behind a cabinet.*

*Short Kid: "Here's what we're gonna do, we're gonna take out all these motherfuckers!"*

*Short Kid stood up and began firing the blaster at all the troops in the room, not missing a single shot! Short Kid was running around all over the room taking cover while repeatedly firing his blaster! The troops kept missing their shots!*

*"DAMN IT HE'S TOO SHORT, OUR SHOTS KEEP GOING OVER HIS HEAD!"*

*Damaris peeked over the cabinet and shot the troop who said that!*

*Damaris: "Sorry!"*

*Short Kid: "Don't fucking say sorry Damaris fuck that troop!"*

*The last two troops tried to run up on the boys, but they luckily shot them before they did anything!*

*Damaris: "Well, looks like we took them all out!"*

*Short Kid: "Yeah, but okay, let's find a way out of this damn ship!"*

*They both ran out the room to find a way to escape! Meanwhile back on the ground, the crew was faced off with Cynthia! She took out a blaster and had it pointed at all of them!*

*Cynthia: "Nobody make a move!"*

*Ms. Garcia: "You're a monster!"*

*Cynthia: "Ok you know what, just for saying that I'm going to kill you all right now!"*

*She put her finger on the trigger and was about to pull it.*

*Cynthia: "Say goodbye you dumb kids!"*

*The gang braced themselves for what was about to happen. When all of a sudden, Murphy came running up from behind Cynthia and shot her with the blaster he stole! He hit his future wife right in her back, and she fell to the ground! She turned her head around while she laid on the ground slowly dying.*

*Cynthia: "M... Murphy? Is that really you?"*

*Murphy: "Yo who the fuck are you?"*

*Cynthia: "Who would have ever thought I would die, at the hands of my husband..."*

*Riley: "What is this bitch talking about?"*

*Marcus: "I know so stupid."*

*As she took her last breath, the crew saw a SUV speeding up and running into troops!*

*Natasha: "IT'S THE CRUISER!"*

*He sped up to them as fast as he could! The doors all opened, and he screamed at them!*

*The Cruiser: "GET IN THE WHIP, MORE OF THESE PORTALS ARE OPENING UP!"*

*Riley turned her head right when she saw more portals opening! Many more troops were emerging!*

*Natasha: "Riley get in!"*

*She pulled her in the SUV and The Cruiser stomped his foot on the gas!*

*The Cruiser: "Oh shit! That's it, I'm driving us out of the city!"*

*Marcus: "Bro, some of our friends are still out here!"*

*Riley: "Yeah!"*

*Natasha: "We need to go help them!"*

*The Cruiser: "Are you crazy? DO YOU NOT SEE WHAT'S GOING ON OUTSIDE?!"*

*Out the window they saw these fighter jets shooting at buildings, Troops breaking into homes, arresting and harming bystanders, and setting everything on fire!*

*Jared: "OH NAH!"*

*Riley: "OH MY GOSH!"*

*Ms. Garcia felt a deep feeling of regret.*

*Ms. Garcia: "Oh no… this is what Randy tried to warn us about."*

*War had officially begun, and the invasion was beginning. Teenage Murphy was sitting in the backseat looking upon what he had thought he wanted just a little while ago. "I can't believe this… this is all my fault. I am so sorry grandpa." he thought to himself.*

*The Cruiser: "WE NEED TO GO NOW IF YOU WANT TO LIVE!"*

*Murphy knew what he had to do, he needed to stop his future self, but didn't know exactly what to do yet. So, he acted a bit crazy in this moment.*

*Murphy: "TAKE US TO THEODORE TOWER NOW!"*

*The Cruiser: "I SAID NO!"*

*Murphy: "THAT'S IT!"*

*He pulled out his blaster and pointed it at The Cruiser.*

*Murphy: "I SAID TAKE US THERE NOW, WE AREN'T LEAVING ANYONE BEHIND!"*

*The Cruiser saw through the mirror he had the blaster pointed at his head.*

*The Cruiser: "Shit... FINE!"*

*He made a left turn and began driving back over there, trying to avoid troops, gunfire, and explosions! Meanwhile, back at the tower, PyroManiac, Author, and Randy had Future Murphy trapped, he was unable to move!*

*Randy: "GIVE UP!"*

*Future Murphy: "HA!"*

*He broke free of all of them, and he individually threw them one by one across the entire room. They were all hurting bad.*

*Author: "Dude, I think I fractured a rib!"*

*Future Murphy slowly walked over to them.*

*Future Murphy: "Give up, you are no match for my incredible strength!"*

*Author: "Let me guess... Ah!"*

*His side was hurting bad, but he still wanted to crack a joke.*

*Author: "Did Marcus give you steroids so you could become that strong?"*

*Future Murphy: "NOW IS NOT THE TIME FOR JOKES!"*

*Randy: "You are sorta right Author, the rumor back in my time was he drank some lab made syrup that gave him his strength!"*

*Author: "HA, I knew it!"*

*Future Murphy: "NO!"*

*Future Murphy: "ENOUGH-!"*

*Before he came at them, Future Murphy stopped for one moment and listened in to his earpiece. The troops speaking to him through his communicator broke news to him.*

*"Sir, I regret to inform you that, your wife has died."*

*After he heard that, his body became full of rage! Without hesitation, he said something crazy.*

*Future Murphy: "You know what, our big ship in the sky, DEPLOY ALL OF IT'S BOMBS, BLOW EVERYTHING AWAY!"*

*PyroManiac: "No! No! No! No!"*

*Future Murphy: "Listen kids, this has been fun."*

*Randy: "HEY, I'M ACTUALLY 25!"*

*Author: "Oh so you're the same age as Ms. Garcia?"*

*Future Murphy: "ENOUGH OF THE STUPID BANTER!"*

*A black helicopter flew next to the window of the floor they were on. Future Murphy noticed and smiled.*

*Future Murphy: "Well, here's my ride, I'm outta here!"*

*Author saw Pyro was ready to keep fighting, and he put his hand on his shoulder.*

*Author: "Hold up bro, take a breather."*

*Future Murphy ran towards the window and jumped through the glass! He grabbed on to the helicopter and it then flew away!*

*Future Murphy: "ENJOY THE SHOW!"*

*PyroManiac: "He got away...."*

*Author: "I know, but Pyro, don't focus on him, he's going to start blowing shit up any second!"*

*Randy: "Yes, please go help the rest of the crew, and anyone else who needs help!"*

*He ran towards the window to go and prepare himself to fly away and find the crew. But before he did, he turned his back and looked at The Author and nodded his head. PyroManiac then flew off and began to look for the crew before any bombs went off!*

*Author: "Okay Randy, grab me, and let's fly up towards his helicopter!"*

*Randy: "Alright!"*

*He grabbed The Author's blazer, picked him up off the ground and they began to fly and chase the helicopter using the jetpack! Bullets coming from the planes in the sky were nearly missing them!*

*Author: "AHHH!"*

*Randy: "HOLD ON!"*

*Meanwhile, back on the ship, Damaris and The Short Kid were running through the ship taking out anyone who stood in their way! As they were running, Short Kid stopped and pointed towards a sign that was hung up.*

*Short Kid: "Damaris look at the sign, it says an exit is to our left."*

*All of a sudden, they heard a voice over an intercom say out loud...*

*"Attention, Murphy has commanded us to prepare to release all our explosives we have on board onto the city!"*

*Damaris: "WHAT?!"*

*Short Kid: "DUDE THEY ARE GOING TO BLOW EVERYTHING UP!"*

*Damaris: "Short Kid, I'm about to panic..."*

*Short Kid: "This is war..."*

*Damaris: "I know..."*

*Short Kid: "There has to be a way we can stop this."*

*Damaris looked at the sign and something caught his attention.*

*Damaris: "Look bro, it says the cockpit of this ship is right down the hall!"*

*Short Kid: "Holy shit."*

*Damaris: "We gotta stop this shit somehow."*

*Short Kid: "What are you thinking bro..."*

*Damaris: "We are right above the lake, right?"*

*Short Kid: "Yeah we are..."*

*Damaris: "Dude..."*

*Short Kid: "Bro Damaris, I know what you're thinking right now, and that is crazy."*

*Damaris: "WE HAVE NO OTHER OPTION!"*

*Short Kid: "I don't know..."*

*Damaris: "UGH, okay listen, you don't think I would rather be at home right now eating buffalo wings, I wish I wasn't here, but I am. We are over 33 thousand feet high up in the sky in a fucking weird spaceship thing, that is about to kill tons of people right now!"*

*Short Kid: "Okay, fine, you didn't have to lecture me."*

*Damaris: "Whatever, and look, there is parachutes over there in that box, we'll jump out of here before it crashes!"*

*Short Kid: "Fine, let's take over and control this damn thing and crash it. But I hope you know if anyone ever finds out about this, they'll make fun of me. This is such a stereotype of my culture."*

*Damaris: "Who cares?! We can save a lot of people right now, but we need to move fast!"*

*Short Kid: "Okay bro, let's do this then!"*

*They ran to the box and grabbed themselves each a parachute and put it on their backs. They heard another announcement over the intercom stating...*

*"25 SECONDS UNTIL WE START SENDING DOWN THE BOMBS!"*

*Damaris: "CRAP!"*

*Short Kid: "Let's move!"*

*They ran towards the cockpit, and once they got to the door, they barged in! The only person in there was the pilot.*

*"WHAT THE?"*

*Short Kid pointed the blaster at him.*

*Short Kid: "Move!"*

*The pilot put his hands up in the air and walked away! Then, it all began. The bottom of the ship opened up, and bombs began to fall down into the city!*

*Damaris: "OH SHIT HURRY!"*

*Back on the ground, The Cruiser was running down troops with the crew on their way back to Theodore Tower, when he noticed something falling from the sky.*

*The Cruiser: "What are all those things falling from that ship up there?"*

*Riley looked out the window, and she knew exactly what they were!*

*Riley: "OH MY GOD, THOSE ARE BOMBS!"*

*The crew all began to panic as they realized they were all about to be blown up!*

*Jared: "OH SHIT!"*

*Natasha: "WE ARE GONNA DIE!"*

*Marcus stuck his head out the window and saw a bomb was about to fall directly on them!*

*Marcus: "AHHH!"*

*It was about to hit the car! Their lives were about to end in a few seconds. Luckily for them, PyroManiac flew underneath the bomb and stopped it from hitting them! He used his body to shield them from the explosion!*

*Murphy: "Whoa, that dude just took a bomb to the chest!"*

*PyroManiac was not hurt by the bomb. The fire from the bomb was attached to his body, and the flames were flowing in the wind. The Cruiser stopped the SUV, and the crew jumped out and ran over to Pyro.*

*Jared: "Yo you good man?"*

*PyroManiac: "Yeah."*

*They looked on as the bombs fell down all across the city! The bombs were hitting many buildings, and everything in sight was being destroyed! They all looked on in horror.*

*Riley: "No... this is terrible!"*

*Fire, screams, and explosions is all that they saw and heard in that moment. It was a nightmare.*

*Marcus: "The city is being destroyed!"*

*Ms. Garcia began to tear up as she looked upon the battlefield they stood in. Back on the ship...*

*Damaris: "OKAY PULL DOWN ON THIS LEVER TO SEND THE SHIP DOWN INTO THE RIVER!"*

*Short Kid: "OKAY I AM!"*

*They pulled down on the steering lever with all their force! The ship began to sink its nose down, and the entire ship began to crash!*

*Damaris: "OH SHIT IT'S WORKING!"*

*Since the ship was leaning forward, the rest of the bombs that were dropping from the bottom of the ship began dropping down into the lake!*

*Riley: "Guys look, the ship is crashing down!"*

*Jared: "Yeah, and the bombs aren't falling onto us anymore!"*

*The bombs were landing in the water exploding!*

*Natasha: "Aw those poor fishes."*

*The Author and Randy were watching this from the sky while they were still going after Future Murphy.*

*Randy: "Wow!"*

*Author: "How is that happening?"*

*The entire ship was leaning forward and was falling down at an extremely fast speed! The ship was about to soon crash into the water!*

*Short Kid: "OKAY IT'S TIME TO GO!"*

*Damaris: "OKAY!"*

*The ship was zooming face down, and the boys had to be careful. Damaris kicked open a window in the cockpit and looked over at Short Kid.*

*Damaris: "YOU READY?"*

*Short Kid: "I GUESS SO!"*

*They took a deep breath and JUMPED OUT OF THE SHIP! Short Kid and Damaris were flying through the air!*

*Short Kid: "AHHHHH!"*

*Damaris: "PULL THE CORD!"*

*They both pulled their parachute cord, and the parachute deployed! It shot them up in the air for a moment, but it kept them up in the air safe. The ship came crashing down into the lake and it exploded!*

*Short Kid: "WE DID IT!"*

*Damaris: "HELL YEAH WE DID!"*

*The crew on foot saw them floating down!*

*Natasha: "THAT WAS AWESOME!"*

*Ms. Garcia: "YAY DAMARIS AND SHORT KID!"*

*The boys were smiling as they were coming down!*

*Damaris: "Come on bro, let's glide ourselves over there, but this still isn't over yet!"*

*Short Kid: "Bet bro!"*

*Back on the ground, Murphy got the crews attention.*

*Murphy: "Let's hurry up, we are about a block away from Theodore Tower!"*

*They all began to run over as fast as they could! Meanwhile, Randy was still carrying The Author up in the air trying to catch Future Murphy in the helicopter.*

*Randy: "He's straight ahead!"*

*Author: "Hand me your blaster, I'll take a shot!"*

*Randy dropped his blaster down to Author and he caught it! He aimed at the helicopter and took a shot at it!*

*Randy: "SHOOT IT AGAIN!"*

*He took a few more shots at it when smoke began to come out of it!*

*Future Murphy: "DAMNIT!"*

*One of the troops sitting in the helicopter handed Future Murphy a blaster! He stuck his head out of the damaged helicopter and took a shot directly at Randy!*

*Randy: "AH!"*

*He shot him in the shoulder!*

*Randy: "SHIT!"*

*Blood was gushing out his shoulder! He began to suddenly feel weak and was losing his strength. He had to fly over and carry The Author to the roof of a random building! He dropped him on the roof, and he sat down and held his wound.*

*Randy: "FUCK!"*

*Author: "Are you okay Randy?"*

*Randy: "It hurts!"*

*Author: "We have to stop him!"*

*Randy: "I know, but I can't keep carrying you, I can barely carry myself right now…"*

*Author: "What do we do then?"*

*Randy then took off his jetpack and threw it down in front of The Author.*

*Randy: "The commander told me you were the one, and he was right."*

*The Author felt overwhelmed for a moment.*

*Randy: "You can stop him, Author."*

*Author: "Are you sure about this?"*

*Randy: "Of course I am, you are a hero."*

*The Author was nervous but knew what had to be done.*

*Randy: "Go get that motherfucker and save the world!"*

*The Author put on the jetpack and grabbed his blaster. He noticed a black bandana that was laying on the roof. He grabbed it and folded it and tied it over his forehead, and his long hair was dangling over it. He put his brass knuckles on and was ready to fight.*

*Author: "I will. The world isn't going to crumble tonight."*

*He turned on the jetpack and began to slowly fly up. The Author saluted Randy, then he turned his jetpack on to the fastest level and flew off towards the helicopter!*

*Author: "I'm coming for you bastard!"*

*Future Murphy saw him from afar!*

*Future Murphy: "I've had enough of this kid trying to get in the way of my plan!"*

*He sent out a message over his communicator!*

*Future Murphy: "TROOPS, OPEN A NEW PORTAL, AND UNLEASH PROJECT 83 ONTO THE CITY!"*

*Someone responded to him.*

*"Right away sir!"*

*Future Murphy: "Great."*

*The Author flew inside of the helicopter at full speed and whipped Future Murphy in the face with his blaster!*

*Future Murphy: "AH DAMN IT!"*

*He tried to grab The Author, but he flew out the door. He shot the engine a few more times, and that's when the helicopter began to plummet to the ground! The pilot began to panic!*

*"Sir, we're going down!"*

*Future Murphy: "I can see that!"*

*They came crashing down at a fast speed, and they crashed into the ground, and the helicopter exploded! The Author looked on from the sky.*

*Author: "He's gone."*

*He flew down to go inspect the wreck. He got close up to the fire and stood still for a minute. Before he realized it, he felt a tight grip around his arm and was pulled down onto the ground! He looked at the person who did it, and Future Murphy was still alive!*

*Author: "Shit!"*

*He couldn't believe that he had survived the crash! Then, Future Murphy slammed his fist down into The Author's chest as hard as he could! He took all the air out of him! He luckily escaped and flew away! Meanwhile, Damaris and The Short Kid safely landed nearby.*

*Damaris: "Well that was a nice ride down."*

*Short Kid: "Yeah, I enjoyed it. I hope PyroManiac saw what we did."*

*Damaris: "Alright now let's focus."*

*Damaris spoke through the communicator.*

*Damaris: "Hey, does anyone copy, what's going on?"*

*Natasha picked up and responded.*

*Natasha: "Hey are you guys okay? That was crazy what you did! But anyway, we're running through the streets right now!"*

*Her and the crew were running to Theodore Tower, while Pyro and Murphy were stopping any troops that got in their way!*

*Damaris: "Okay, where are you going?!"*

*Natasha: "We're going to-!"*

*Marcus jumped on the line and started speaking!*

*Marcus: "Natasha, you're not going to believe this, look behind you!"*

*Natasha: "What?"*

*She looked behind her and saw a tank coming straight at them!*

*Natasha: "OH SHIT A TANK!"*

*Pyro saw the tank coming up on them, so he flew over to it and was about to destroy it!*

*Marcus: "WAIT NO!"*

*The lid of the tank opened up and Marcus popped out! He was inside driving it!*

*Marcus: "I stole a tank."*

*The crew was pretty confused.*

*Natasha: "How the hell did you steal a tank?"*

*Marcus: "It was easy, basically I-!"*

*Natasha: "Forget I even asked, but whatever it's good we have that equipment."*

*She hopped back on the communicator.*

*Natasha: "Sorry about that Damaris, we're heading over to Theodore Tower, we just saw a helicopter crash over there, and we can't get ahold of The Author or Randy."*

*Damaris: "Okay, we're heading over there now!"*

*He looked over to Short Kid and said to him "Let's hurry!" But as they were about to run over there, a giant portal began to emerge from behind them!*

*Short Kid: "Oh shit what is it now?!"*

*The portal had fully formed, and the boys stood there in anticipation of what was about to come through. Then suddenly, a swarm of what appeared to be green, rabid raccoons jumped out of the portal and began hissing aggressive!*

*Short Kid: "What the hell are those?"*

*One of the came up to them and stared at them with its bright red eyes and super sharp teeth.*

*Damaris: "They look like, zombie raccoons?!"*

*The raccoon jumped up and almost bit Damaris! Luckily he hit it with the blaster!*

*Short Kid: "DON'T LET THEM BITE YOU, THEY MIGHT BE INFECTED WITH SOMETHING!"*

*Hundreds of these zombie raccoons began emerging out of the portal, and all the green little monsters began to chase after the boys!*

*Damaris: "RUN DUDE!"*

*They both took off as fast as they could! Meanwhile the crew was nearby where The Author was! They kept running as fast as they could because the fighter jets in the sky kept shooting down at them! Marcus inside the tank, had enough of one of the planes shooting down at his friends, so he aimed the barrel of the tank up at the sky and shot a cannon at one of the planes and it hit! The plane was struck and came crashing down in a million pieces!*

*Marcus: "They shouldn't have kept playing like that!"*

*Just down the street from them, the fight continued between The Author and Future Murphy. The Author took out his knife, and flew up to him, then slashed him in the face! Future Murphy put his hand over his face and felt the blood oozing from his face!*

*Future Murphy: "YOU'RE GOING TO DIE!"*

*He flew up from behind him and kicked the back of his head!*

*Future Murphy: "Ah!"*

*The Author flew up to him again and was about to throw a punch at him, but this time he caught Author's fist, and broke his wrist!*

*Author: "OH MY GOD MY WRIST!"*

*Future Murphy kneed The Author in the face, and he fell to the ground! He then kicked him a few times, picked him up, and threw him through a glass window of a building! The Author was in so much pain, and he tried to fly away, but the jetpack was crushed and destroyed!*

*Author: "Shit."*

*Murphy came up to him and punched his body again, he picked him up again and threw him near a dumpster. At that moment, he knew he was done for.*

*Author: "I can't move… fuck… I'm hurt too bad."*

*Meanwhile as Damaris and Short Kid were running away from the zombie raccoons, they realized they weren't going to be able to get away!*

*Damaris: "FUCK WE NEED TO HIDE!"*

*Short Kid: "I can't run much more!"*

*As they were running, Damaris saw a bakery and said, "Go in here!" They opened the door inside, and barricaded the door before any of the zombie raccoons could get to them! They were surrounding the entire building!*

*Damaris: "Well, we're trapped in here now!"*

*They heard explosions coming from outside! Tanks kept shooting at random buildings, and gunfire kept coming down from the sky!*

*Short Kid: "I really wish I was at home with my family..."*

*Damaris: "Me too."*

*Damaris sighed.*

*Short Kid: "All we can do now is pray bro."*

*Damaris: "I agree."*

*The glass on the window of the bakery began to crack as more of the evil raccoons were trying to get through! The boys began to accept their fate... The rest of the crew was running up on Future Murphy! Natasha screamed out at him!*

*Natasha: "HEY ASSHOLE, WE'RE HERE TO STOP YOU!"*

*PyroManiac began to fly straight at Future Murphy while the rest of the crew followed behind him. Murphy and Riley snuck up and hid behind a pile of* debris near where The Author was laying. Future Murphy smiled, because he knew what was exactly about to happen. A giant portal opened up in between him and the crew! A huge plane came zooming out of the portal, smashing into The PyroManiac!

Natasha: "OH NO!"

The impact of the hit sent The PyroManiac flying! His body got tossed across the city and his body crashed into a random building! He momentarily became unconscious. Then dozens of more troops came rushing out of the portal, and pointed their guns at Jared, The Cruiser, Ms. Garcia, and Natasha! A few of the troops ambushed the tank and pulled Marcus out of it!

"All of you, put your hands in the air, you are under arrest and will now serve and obey MURPHY!"

With no other option, they all complied, and the troops began to put handcuffs on them all. The Author was barely conscious when all of this was going on.

Riley: "Murphy, you have to stop them!"

Murphy: "How?!"

Riley: "I DON'T KNOW!"

Murphy: "Shhh, keep your voice down, we don't want him to see us."

*Riley: "Yeah, that guy you refer to as him, that's you."*

*She meant it as a sarcastic comment, but Murphy took it to heart what she said. It was his future self doing all of this destruction. There must be a way he could stop himself. He looked around and saw what once was a beautiful city, crumbling down, on fire, people hurt and dead, and troops were taking over... it was awful. But it clicked in his mind, Murphy knew that there was only one thing left he could do to stop all of this.*

*Murphy: "I know what I have to do."*

*Riley looked at him confused.*

*Murphy: "Riley, the only way to change the future, is to change the past..."*

*At that moment, she realized what he meant. They kept hiding as Future Murphy began speaking.*

*Future Murphy: "I find it hilarious you all thought you could stop me! This isn't even a quarter of my army! This is only the beginning of the invasion!"*

*They all listened on.*

*Future Murphy: "And now, you will all witness the death of your leader, The Author!"*

*Marcus: "NOO!"*

*"Shut the fuck up!"*

227

*A troop hit Marcus in the face!*

*Future Murphy: "Say goodbye!"*

*He faced The Author as he was laying on the ground in pain. He slowly walked up to him, and grabbed the blaster out of his pocket, then spit on him!*

*Author: "Ew."*

*He took a few feet back and pointed the blaster directly at his head.*

*Future Murphy: "Say your prayers, Author."*

*He put his finger on the trigger, and all of his friends were screaming!*

*Natasha: "NO PLEASE!"*

*Ms. Garcia: "AUTHOR!!"*

*The Author sat there as he saw a future version of his best friend, about to shoot him. He had a huge smile on his face, and The Author braced himself for what was about to come...*

*\*BOOM\**

*Everything was pitch black, and silent. Nobody was making any noise. For a second, The Author thought he was dead. Until he realized, he had not been shot. He heard a loud thud, and he opened his eyes. He saw Future Murphy with his jaw wide open. He had the most shocked look on his face.*

*He dropped the blaster onto the ground and froze! The crew who was watching this all go down was shocked! Riley stood up from behind the debris and looked on to what just happened! That's when The Author realized what happened...*

*Author: "Oh my god."*

*Murphy had jumped in front of the shot! The Author got up quickly and looked down at his best friend. Murphy was hurt bad.*

*Author: "OH MY GOD MURPHY!"*

*He opened his eyes, and The Author grabbed his hand. His injury was clearly fatal.*

*Murphy: "Thank you for giving me a second chance, I love you, you my day one."*

*Author: "Bro..."*

*Murphy smiled at his friend.*

*Murphy: "Always do the right thing, even if it hurts..."*

*He slowly slipped away. His hand became limp, and tears began to run down The Author's face.*

*Author: "Murphy..."*

*The crew was in disbelief. They couldn't comprehend what they had just saw. The Author looked up at Future Murphy in tears.*

*Author: "I tried to save you."*

*He stood there as he realized that he just murdered his teenage self. And he knew that, without the past, there is no present.*

*Future Murphy: "I've failed."*

*He began to slowly disappear into thin air, as if he never existed. And so did everything else, all the troops, the tanks, planes, and zombie raccoons, all just faded away. As Randy sat on the roof, he was in disbelief when he saw all the fighter jets fade away.*

*Randy: "The future is saved."*

*All the troops disappeared that were surrounding the crew, and their handcuffs vanished too!*

*Ms. Garcia: "This is incredible."*

*PyroManiac had woken up, he stood up and saw that all the tanks and troops were dissolving into nothing. He was shocked. Damaris and Short Kid walked out of the bakery and saw it all disappear.*

*Damaris: "Bro, look around us!"*

*Short Kid: "Damaris, the war is over."*

*All the damage and destruction that had been caused that night, had disappeared and returned to its original state. The destruction of the bombs, canons, fire, had all faded away.*

*Natasha: "It's like witnessing a miracle."*

*Then, all of their wounds and injuries healed up instantly. All of their broken bones, gunshot wounds, cuts and bruises all healed immediately.*

*Marcus: "I don't get it, what's happening?"*

*Randy came up from behind Marcus and talked to him.*

*Randy: "Murphy didn't get to grow old enough to become Evil Murphy. The timeline has changed, without a past, there can be no future. So, all of the damage and destruction he brought basically never existed."*

*Marcus: "Woah, trippy."*

*The boys came running up to the rest of the crew!*

*Jared: "Damaris and Short Kid I'm glad you guys are okay!"*

*The three of them hugged!*

*Any bystanders or other people around who were harmed or killed were healed and revived!*

*"I can't believe it! I thought I was dead!"*

*PyroManiac came flying down to regroup with the crew!*

*PyroManiac: "What happened?!"*

*Randy: "We won."*

*Even though they were happy, they realized at what cost this came at for The Author. They all looked down at him and saw him on the ground bawling his eyes out. His best friend for the past 18 years was now gone. Riley moved everyone out the way and hugged Author. She tried to comfort him as much as possible.*

*Riley: "I'm so sorry Author."*

*While this may have ended up being the inevitable, it was commendable the sacrifice Murphy made to save not only his friend, but the whole world. Everyone was heartbroken. The Author stood up and was destroyed.*

*Author: "Thank you gang, for everything."*

*He smiled at all of them and had a few more tears come down his face.*

*Author: "Go home and go get some rest."*

*He turned on the jetpack and went flying off!*

*The Cruiser: "I wonder where he's going?"*

*"Hey look!"*

*"Those are the kids that saved us!"*

*A large group of people gathered around them and began cheering for them! They were seen as heroes!*

*Natasha: "They love us!"*

*The people outside were cheering and people began taking pictures of them! That's when the media showed up! The crew didn't notice, but PyroManiac went to go hide in the shadows to avoid the crowd.*

1 hoUR
LATER

*It was 5:20 AM, the sun was rising, and the air felt amazing outside. The Author was sitting on the edge of a tall building in the city. He was drinking a cup of coffee and eating a bacon, egg and cheese sandwich. He was processing everything that just happened to him. He didn't think anyone would find him up there, but he was wrong. PyroManiac came flying up and landed his feet on the roof.*

*PyroManiac: "Sup."*

*Author: "Oh, hey Pyro."*

*He walked towards The Author. He sat down next to him and The Author sat there zoned out as he saw the sun come up.*

*Author: "It's crazy, I felt like I wasn't ever going to see the sun again."*

*PyroManiac: "I've been there before."*

*The Author felt a bulge in his blazer pocket. He reached his hand in there and pulled out that blunt he took from Murphy's desk.*

*Author: "I forgot I even had this."*

*He was surprised it wasn't damaged at all.*

*Author: "Damn I would smoke this right now, but I don't have a lighter!"*

*Pyro grabbed it from him and lit it with his finger.*

*Author: "Thank you."*

*He took a deep inhale and let it all out while taking a sip of coffee.*

*Author: "You want some bro?"*

*PyroManiac: "Why not?"*

*At that moment, he put his hands on his mask and took it off. He lifted his head up, and for the first time The Author saw what he looked like under the scary looking mask.*

*Author: "Wow, you're just a kid like me, I thought you were like 30?!"*

*PyroManiac: "Haha, nah, I'm 18."*

*The Author passed Pyro the blunt and he also took a puff.*

*PyroManiac: "My real name is Ethan though."*

*Author: "Wow, that is a dope ass name, super unique."*

*PyroManiac: "It's fuckin' common."*

*Author: "Haha, true. But hey man, I did want to say thank you for helping me out with all this stuff. Truthfully, we probably would have died like 6 times if it weren't for you."*

*Ethan: "No problem, man."*

*Ethan took a huge hit with no cough. Since fire is in his DNA, the heat and ash from the blunt didn't affect him like that. The Author turned and looked at him in a "Goddamn!" type of way.*

*Ethan: "Shit's strong."*

*Author: "Yeah, Murphy would not go with any of that cheap shit."*

*The Author sighed when he said his name.*

*Author: "Damn, that was my homie since I was a baby... I'm going to miss that dude so much."*

*Ethan: "Murphy was able to save so many people with his sacrifice, and you ended things on good terms with him."*

*Author: "Yeah bro, you're right."*

*Ethan: "And if it weren't for you, he wouldn't have done that. You know you saved the world, right?"*

*He passed the blunt back to The Author.*

*Author: "I don't know bro."*

*Ethan: "The media is gonna look at you like a hero now."*

*Author: "Damn, you for real think that?"*

*Ethan: "Of course. But don't get too comfortable with the hero shit, you've seen the headlines about me!"*

*Ethan laughs a bit.*

*Ethan: "But whatever you do with your future, I wish you the best of luck."*

*Author: "Thank you, I appreciate that."*

*He hit the blunt a few more times and passed it back to Ethan. The Author stood up and cracked his back.*

*Author: "Alright man I think ima try and find a way home."*

*Ethan nodded, and finished the blunt, and the two men had a firm handshake. They each had mutual respect for one another.*

*Ethan: "What you gonna do when you get home?"*

*Author: "I'm going to take a long nap."*

*Ethan walked towards the edge of the building and put his mask back on.*

*Author: "Wait before you go, what are you gonna do now?"*

*PyroManiac: "I got some stuff I have to take care of. I'll see you around, Author."*

*Author: "See ya bro."*

*He turned around and flew off of the building! The Author watched him fly away. He stood up and took one last look at the city before he went home...*

# SATURDAY

*Teenage Heroes Defeat Time-Traveling Menace, Saving the World from Future Murphy's Reign of Terror!*

"In a breathtaking display of bravery and self-sacrifice, a group of extraordinary teenagers emerged as the unlikely saviors of our world. Their valiant efforts thwarted the sinister plans of a man known as Future Murphy, who had traveled back in time with a formidable army, threatening to rewrite history and plunge humanity into darkness. The night was filled with chaos and destruction as Future Murphy unleashed an arsenal of troops, tanks, fighter jets, and even zombie raccoons upon unsuspecting citizens. Panic gripped the world as hope seemed to fade away. However, amidst the turmoil, 12 young adults, some with advanced abilities and utilities, rose to the occasion, determined to protect the future of humanity. But victory came at a great cost. As the battle raged on, Future Murphy aimed a fatal shot at The Author. In a twist of fate, Murphy from the past, driven by a newfound understanding of the consequences, leaped in front of the bullet, sacrificing himself to save the future.

As the past altered, Future Murphy's existence ceased, erasing his army and undoing his malevolent plans in the process. In the wake of this monumental sacrifice, the world breathed a collective sigh of relief. The heroic group of teenagers had succeeded in rewriting destiny and preventing the calamitous future that awaited them. Their selfless actions had not only saved countless lives but also united people globally in an outpouring of gratitude and admiration. The Author, The Short Kid, Riley, Natasha, Damaris, The Cruiser, Marcus, Jared, Ms. Garcia, Natasha, Randy, and The PyroManiac, are now celebrated as true heroes. Their names have become synonymous with courage and resilience, and their story has captivated hearts around the world. Today, as humanity basks in the aftermath of their triumph, the world stands in awe of these extraordinary individuals. They have proven that even in the face of insurmountable odds, hope can prevail, and ordinary people can achieve extraordinary feats. This legend will forever inspire future generations, reminding us that heroism is not limited by age but driven by the indomitable spirit of humanity."

*When The Author walked across the graduation stage and accepted his diploma, everyone in the audience clapped and cheered. For the first time in his life, he actually felt accepted by people. The members of his crew that were graduating were also heavily cheered for! Everyone in the country was talking about them! It all felt surreal. But the one thing that bothered The Author was the empty chair next to him, that was meant for Murphy. He walked out the building, and everyone wanted to talk to him. He talked to them, but deep down he felt dead inside. Afterwards, him and Riley talked outside after the ceremony.*

*Author: "Listen, I love you so much, but I think right now I just want to be alone."*

*Riley: "What?"*

*Author: "I don't want to end things with you. But I just need a break for myself. You know, all of our physical scars disappeared, but our emotional ones didn't."*

*Riley: "Hey look I understand."*

*Author: "You do?"*

*Riley: "Of course."*

*Author: "Thank you, and I still want you to come to the dinner tonight."*

*Riley: "I'll see you then."*

*The night came, and him, Damaris, Short Kid, Riley, Natasha, Jared, Marcus, Ms. Garcia, Cruiser, and Randy all went out to dinner.*

*Damaris: "I can't believe we graduated!"*

*Short Kid: "Yeah and now look at us!"*

*Ms. Garcia: "Every media outlet is talking about us."*

*Jared: "It's wild."*

*Marcus: "Not as wild as the baddies who keep coming up to me at the gym."*

*The Cruiser: "HAHA!"*

*Natasha: "My grandparents called me freaking out!"*

*Riley: "SAME WITH MINE!"*

*They all laughed as they were eating their Italian food. Randy was scarfing down his bowl of pasta!*

*Randy: "Wow! Food taste so much better than it did in the future!"*

*Author: "So Randy, what are you going to do now about everything?"*

*He finished slurping down his pasta and reached into his back pocket and pulled out a device.*

*Randy: "I had time last night to fix up the device that sent me here in the first place."*

*Short Kid: "Wow that's cool."*

*Ms. Garcia: "Yeah that is cool..."*

*She looked over at Randy and smiled.*

*Randy: "Thank you."*

*They both began to blush.*

*Natasha: "Uh, what's going on here?"*

*Ms. Garcia: "Oh my gosh, nothing!"*

*Randy: "Yeah nothing... but I do think you are...."*

*Ms. Garcia: "Think I'm what?"*

*Randy: "Cute."*

*Damaris: "Oh shit Randy with the rizz!"*

*Ms. Garcia: "Well Randy, even though I just met you a few days ago under strange circumstances, I think your handsome."*

*The kids were all blushing and laughing as they saw this all unfold. The Author felt secondhand embarrassment!*

*Randy: "Listen, I'd like to go out sometime."*

*Ms. Garcia: "I'd like that."*

*Jared: "YESSIR!"*

*Marcus: "THAT'S WHAT'S UP!"*

*Randy stood up and turned on the device.*

*Randy: "I'm going to go and check out some different time periods, but I'll be back in a little bit if that's okay?"*

*Ms. Garcia smiled.*

*Ms. Garcia: "Be safe out there, and don't cause any trouble."*

*He turned on the device and it began to slowly transport him.*

*Randy: "Thank you again, Author."*

*Author: "No problem, I'll see you later!"*

*He waved goodbye and faded away into the bright light!*

*Riley: "Wow that was magical."*

*The Cruiser: "Hold up did that dude pay for his food?"*

*They noticed that he didn't pay for his meal.*

*Jared: "Shit."*

■■■■■■■■■■■■■■■■■■■■■■■■■■■■■■■■■■■■■■■■■■■■■■■■

*The crew all spoke after Randy left. They had come to terms that now since high school was over, they would all be going their own separate ways in life now. The Author knew this was coming, but it all happened so fast. Natasha and Riley will be doing their own things from now on. Ms. Garcia is gonna wait for Randy to come back and keep doing the political stuff. Marcus is going to keep hitting the gym every day, while The Cruiser will still be driving The Author around. Jared, Damaris and The Short Kid will be sticking around, but obviously doing different things with their lives. Even though it was a sad goodbye, everyone will have their own new adventures and stories to create, and hopefully they can come to terms with everything they've experienced these past few days. The Author was sad to see his crew split up, but he knew if the time ever came where the world needed them, they would come back together!*
*The Author was walking home when he threw his graduation cap and gown in a trash can.*

*As he was walking home at night, he thought to himself "I used to see the world all from a teenager's point of view, but now, I truly see everything differently." When he got home and walked upstairs and headed to his bedroom where this story began. He looked on his nightstand and saw the coffee flavored vape Short Kid gave him. He smiled about it, opened his drawer and put it away. But he opened the door back up when a picture sitting in the drawer caught his attention. He grabbed it and stared at the picture. He began to get a little emotional.*

*Author: "This needs to be framed."*

*He put the picture in a frame and hung it up on his wall. He wiped away his tears and smiled.*

*Author: "Thank you for everything bro."*

*He walked away from the photo, and it was a picture of Murphy and him when they were 6 years old, wearing matching shirts that said...*

*Friendship never dies.*

# AIDEN BRANSS BOOKS